A FAMILY AFFAIR
AND
OTHER STORIES

Publications by the author:

Novel, paperback
The Kurdish Episode

Hardback textbook
Three-Phase Electrical Power

This book is a collection of short stories, of which more than half had been published earlier by a variety of publishers.

ISBN 978-1-64570-980-0

Printed in the United States of America

A FAMILY AFFAIR AND OTHER STORIES

Fictional and Narrative Nonfictional

Short Stories

by

Joseph E. Fleckenstein

CONTENTS

So White Plus Seven
The Metzes
Egyptian Pounds
Too-late Dowry
Jim and the Big Black Skunk
A Family Affair
A Subtle Play
Cousin Paul
Novice Bank Robber
Pretend Love
We, the ROTC Cadets
Gobblers and Grapes
The Snow Queen Contest
Henri Rochemont
Roisin
Camping with Friends
Little Pietro
The Yazidis
The Twentieth Reunion
Driving to Work
Sirus
Encounter on Line Mountain
Comes Around
Hamburgers
The Two Mile Club
The Late Train from Alexandria
The Annual Turkey Calling Contest

Appendix

Introduction

In this book I present a collection of twenty-seven short stories, all written by me over the years. The bulk of the pieces are fictional although a few are nonfiction and are written in the creative nonfiction format. Of the fictional stories, all except two are considered literary short stories. "Too-late Dowry" and "Family Affair" fit the classification of genre. The first seventeen stories were published either in print or online by a variety of publishers whereas the remainder have not yet been previously published. All of the published stories were selected by the editorial staffs of publishers. That is significant, given that literary publishers in general are very selective and generally accept less than one percent of all submittals.

I expect readers will detect in my stories an inclination to humor and irony. More or less, that is my style. As far as I am concerned, a story is not a good story unless it contains at least a dash of these ingredients. Both of these traits are embedded in every one of the fictional stories although in some instances to a subtle degree. After all, life is full of irony. Why not shine a light on it? As for humor, you may note that I intertwine it whenever possible.

Thinking that readers might be interested in learning of the origins of the stories, I provide a brief explanation of the events that prompted me to write the respective stories. In some instances those prefaces are stories in their own right. These background stories are included in the appendix for the benefit of those individuals who might have an interest in such matters.

The creative nonfiction stories to a large extent represent true events, although in no case are actual names repeated.   …
,,,, Joseph Fleckenstein

So White plus Seven
(A fictional short story)

Over the past years we noticed kids were losing their interest in our circus. They had their TV's, iPads, computer games. Then it happened! The big boss called the seven of us in. Somil White, the girl who rode the elephant, was there too.

"I'm sorry everyone," the man said. "The Schultz Circus declared bankruptcy this morning. The equipment was bought by a Chinese firm. There's no money to pay you. You can exit through the main door. Security will show you the way."

Bang! Just like that we were on the street with no money and no place to go. Outside the main door, Grumpy picked up a rock and threw it at the big sign with the words "Schultz Circus—Freaks and Wild Animals." When the rock hit, he let out a loud, "You motherfuckers." The rock fell on a garbage can lid, making the sound of cymbals clanging. Much as the final note of a Puccini tragic opera.

Sleepy said he knew of a city park two blocks away.

"Why don't we go there and talk." Somil, who we call "So" for short, said she would like to come along if we all didn't mind. She added, "After all, eight heads are better than one even if some are pretty small."

Dopey looked at me.

"Sneezy, who does the smartass pussy think she is?"

Speaking to no one, and looking at the sky, I said in a loud voice, "Word has it she is the illegitimate daughter of an Indian maharani."

It was true, So came from India. She said her family knew elephants. That's how she got the job. But we all thought the maharani was made up, as in upmanship. She said her family name, "White," came from some Englishman who had been fooling around with her grandmother. That was believable.

We started walking toward the park. Half way there, Sleepy pinched So's behind. He had to jump up to do it since So is tall with long legs and her ass is up high. She swung at him but he juked.

At the park bench, Bashful was the first to speak.

"Hey guys, look at it on the bright side. We are now eligible for unemployment, public housing, and food stamps. You know, no more being the freaks in side shows to make people laugh. Just lounging around, watching TV, and fishing by the river."

Everyone had to agree. Bashful might be on to something. That night we slept in the park. The next morning we combed So's hair and tried our best to make her look pretty. When we were about finished, I stood back and had a look.

"So, these are desperate times. You need to unbutton the top six buttons and get rid of that bra. Let them flop around."

So frowned, pouted and, in a huff, turned to go to the washroom at McDonald's. When she returned we were ready for the Bureau of Public Housing.

So turned on the charm. She told the guy she had "seven little ones" and that she needed a place to stay. Their fathers were not around. Fortunately our whiskers hadn't grown much in one day. Government types are not all that "alert." He figured small people equals children. Besides, he was not looking in our direction. With a smile, but no questions, he gave So a key to an apartment.

After we had an apartment at the Project we applied for unemployment. Having an address, we could tell them where to send the checks. They also gave us a pile of food stamps. Because we are tiny people, except for So, we had more stamps than we could ever use. There were enough to feed So plus 55 dwarves.

All went fairly well the first few weeks at the Project. The apartment had two big beds. So slept in one and everyone else in the other. Sleepy, we learned, was a snorer. Dwarves have small mouths so they don't sound like a big person when they snore. Sleepy sounded more like a pig in heat. Little squeals came one after the other. *Whee...whee...whee.* When he started that noise, Bashful and Grumpy would drag him to the bathroom and push a couch up against the door. In the morning, they would let him out. If anyone had to pee during the night they had to go out the front door and wet the marigolds.

The second week, Happy made some local contacts and found a supplier. He kept swiping our food stamps and trading them for whatever he could obtain. In a way everyone was glad he was mostly stoned and out of the way. Otherwise he was grouchy and a genuine pain.

The TV got to be a problem. There were eight of us and only one TV. Bashful and Doc wanted to watch mysteries. Dopey, Grumpy and Sleepy sitcoms. So, Happy and I the news and the history channel. It was a never-ending contest. One night Bashful wanted to watch Batman. Grumpy said, "no way, Batman's a creep." They went outside. Grumpy came back with a shiner. We all watched Batman.

Bashful resumed his cross-dressing. He had gone to Target where he bought a few girl's dresses, a wig, and lipstick. In the afternoons, he would wander the sidewalks of the Project. One day he returned and was watching Sesame Street. A beer in one hand and a cigarette in the other. A gentle knock was heard on the front door. I went over and opened the door. Two little girls with dolls in their hands stood there.

"Can the little girl come out to play?"

"Little girl?"

"We live in Building C and we saw her come to this apartment."

"Oh, yes. Well, she is having her nap right now. Besides, I don't think you want to play with Bashy. She tends to bite people. Leaves ugly marks."

The girls looked at one another and ran away, screaming.

One night, Sleepy looked at So as she and the others sat watching TV. So was in her PJ's.

"So, we've been here a month now, and we haven't seen you with a boyfriend. You need to get a life."

"Who would want to go around with a chick that has a houseful of midgets? I've been looking for a job, but there is little demand for elephant riders. I'd like to get out of here."

Grumpy took exception to So's comments.

"Well, So, if you don't like living with midgets there is nobody keeping you here. We can get along perfectly well without you. Riding around on your high elephant apparently gave you an attitude."

Because I was fond of So I told Grumpy, "Ah, shut up. We love So and she can stay as long as she likes."

She came over and, reaching down, mussed my hair.

"Sneezy, you're the best."

If only, I thought, my arms were longer. I would have lifted So and threw her on that bed of hers. I would kiss her behind the ear, my hand would wander. So would breath in my ear. We would take our time.

We lived the good life for a time but the unemployment was coming to an end. There were no job prospects in sight. We were all becoming concerned when a Chinese guy came knocking on the door. Very polite but difficult to understand. He said that his employer bought the Schultz Circus and all of the equipment was being shipped to China. He wanted to hire us. And, he said, for 25% above what we were paid by Schultz. He had a contract prepared for each of us. The following week we boarded an Air China 747 for Beijing.

At 35,000 feet the captain announced that supper would be ready in two hours' time. In the meantime, he said, fresh fruit and raw vegetables would be served. In a few minutes a stewardess appeared. Strange looking, though. She had a big mole on her left cheek and a nose that was big for a Chinaman. For some reason she started at our row. I took a pear. So reached over and took the only red apple on the tray.

The Metzes
(A fictional, although partly-true short story)

It was my father's idea. In a letter he suggested I visit our relatives in the village of Lembach. He wrote that the village is in the Vosges Mountains of France. He said they would be happy to see me. It would be a good experience. I had the street address in my pocket.

Finding my way around the mountains proved to be a challenge. It was becoming dark and foggy as well. I knew I was near the village. A few kilometers back I had seen the sign "Lembach." Yet, I started having visions of being obliged to sleep in my small Peugeot rental. Running short on options, I saw a well-kept road off to the right. I drove up the road, but damn it, it ended near a farm house. I was embarrassed as I started to think I was on private property. Turning around, I spotted a man standing behind the house. His back was to me and he had a cigarette in his hand. Thinking he could perhaps help, I exited the car and walked over to him. My guess was that he was a German speaker but I spoke in French nevertheless.

"Excuse me, sir. Sorry to bother you. I am looking for the town of Lembach, but I am having trouble finding the right road."

He was slow to turn around, occupied with his cigarette.

"Oh, yes. You are not far from Lembach."

The man looked at me curiously and took a drag on his cigarette. Letting out smoke he added, "But, the roads from here to Lembach are difficult to follow. Especially at night."

I didn't know what to say, trying to decide on a course of action. I must have blinked my eyes a few times, perhaps displaying hesitation and confusion.

"You are American, I believe?"

"Yes. I had business in Switzerland, but I came here to look-up relatives. According to my father they live in Lembach."

"Interesting. We rarely see Americans around here."

He stamped on his cigarette butt. I figured the man wished to return to his house. It was time for me to depart.

"Thank you sir. I'll give it another try."

He extended his hand.

"My name is Henri Metz."

The handshake was firm but the hand was soft.

"Pleased to meet you, sir. My name is John Gerhart. As you say, Jean Gerhart."

"You have a problem. It is going to be difficult finding Lembach at night and with the fog settling in. We often have fog at this altitude."

"I suppose I should have started earlier. I misjudged the time to drive here."

"Mr. Gerhart, have you eaten this evening?"

"Why, no. I was hoping to find an inn where I might eat and stay for the evening."

"We are having chicken tonight. You are welcome to join us. We can talk more about the road to Lembach. Your auto is fine where you parked it. Nobody will bother it up here."

"Thank you, Mr. Metz. That is very kind of you."

I followed Mr. Metz into his house. It was surprisingly large, made of stone and apparently very old. The windows were fitted with functioning shutters. We went into the kitchen where two women were busy preparing supper. It smelled delicious.

"Ladies, we have a guest tonight. An American traveler."

Mr. Metz introduced me first to the older woman, "Miss Sabine Metz."

"Good evening, sir."

Mr. Metz said Sabine was his niece and the second woman, "Hélène," his daughter. Hélène extended her hand, smiled and, in the European manner, nodded slightly.

I guessed Sabine was in her 40's. Hélène in her mid-30's, roughly my age. Both were svelte and attractive.

Mr. Metz led me into an ante room where he put his hand on a bottle of wine.

"How about an aperitif? Perhaps a Dubonnet?"

"That would be fine. Thank you."

Mr. Metz handed me a glass of Dubonnet.

"You might know. The American Army passed through here during the war. This was my grandfather's house at the time. According to all reports there was fierce fighting around here. During the heat of one battle the family huddled in the wine cellar under the house. The Germans were retreating reluctantly to the east and putting up a good fight as they went. Eventually they had to retreat across the Rhine. Poor fellows. Most were in their mid-teens, mere children. Grandfather put up some 50 American soldiers in this house for a period. He said it was bitter cold. The soldiers were very polite and well behaved. We owe much to the American army."

After two Dubonnets, Sabine came in to announce supper was ready. At the table Hélène sat to my right and Sabine on my left, near the kitchen door. Mr. Metz explained the language situation as, he said, it might seem strange to people from out of the Alsace region.

"Sabine comes from a family that speaks only German and her French is limited. Hélène learned her French in school where German is no longer taught. She speaks French better than German. If she reads a book it will be in French. I speak both

French and German equally well. My ancestors were German speakers for thousands of years. But I was obliged to learn French after the war because my business needs are here in France."

The wine had given me a good appetite and I ate my fill. Perhaps more than what would have been polite. When Mr. Metz was busy with his knife and fork, Hélène cast side glances in my direction. Sometimes she hesitated for an embarrassing period. Once a foot lightly touched my right foot, but it might have accidental.

After supper Mr. Metz guided me back to the ante room where, without asking, he poured two cognacs. The evening was growing late and outside the fog was growing worse. Mr. Metz and I chatted for a time about the war and, in general, the people of Alsace. He was an interesting man and well informed on a range of topics. When the cognac was gone he stood.

"Mr. Gerhart, it's growing late. You would have trouble on the roads with all the fog. Why don't you stay with us tonight. We have ample rooms upstairs."

The invitation from Mr. Metz came as a surprise, but certainly a welcomed one. Mostly because of all of the wine and Cognac, I did not look forward to struggling with the roads on a dark and foggy night in an unfamiliar mountainous region.

"Why, thank you, sir. I appreciate your generosity."

"Not at all."

I retrieved my suitcase from the rental. When I returned to the house Hélène met me inside the door. She told me, "I will show you to your room. It's up the stairs."

She led me to a spacious bedroom that was off a wide hallway.

"The WC is at the end of the hall. You can't miss it."

Pointing to a window over my shoulder she told me, "That window is opened slightly to catch the western air. You may wish to close it if the room becomes too chilly."

I turned to look at the western window. At that instant she walked behind me going to the doorway. I felt a finger drag across my backside.

"Good evening, Mr. Gerhart."

There was a small light in the room so I climbed in bed and started reading a chapter of John Grisham's, "Gray Mountain." Growing drowsy I gave up reading and turned the light off. The room was totally dark. Soon I was dreaming. I found the Gerharts in Lembach. A gorgeous and busty peasant woman in a flimsy dress met me at the door. She said there was nobody home and she was exceedingly happy to meet an American cousin. How wonderful. She led me to their living room, and shortly she brought in a bottle of an Alsatian wine. Soon the wine had its affect. We were talking about America when, for no apparent reason, she came over to me. She said, "Excuse me," and reached behind me to straighten a toile. A firm breast pressed against my forehead. Holding a toile in her hand she stood in front of me, breathing heavily. I took her hand and she led me to a bedroom. As we were bouncing around in bed I heard the front door open. Over her shoulder I saw a large man standing in the doorway holding a pitchfork in his hand. Suddenly, I awoke with a shock. My heart was racing and I was gasping for air. I noticed I was ready for love making. What a disappointment.

After I gathered myself together, I realized my bladder was full and I needed to visit the WC. I couldn't see a thing so I felt for the wall and then moved along until I came to the door. Opening it I realized there was a dim light at the end of the hall. After returning to the bedroom I fell asleep again. But the dream did not resume.

Sometime in the middle of the night, perhaps early morning,

I was awakened by creaking floor boards in the hallway. At first I was unsure that I was actually awake. Perhaps, I thought, I was still dreaming. There was a light tapping on the door and then the door opened slowly. In seconds the blurry outline of a woman was framed in the door. Closing the door behind her, she found her way to the bed and climbed under the sheets with me. I made room and slowly eased my arms around her waist. I tried to kiss her but she did not want to exchange kisses. It was my impression Hélène was intent on getting down to business. She had no panties beneath the pajamas, so that was no problem. I tried to move above her, but that was also not her preference. She intended to be on top, so to speak, in command of the arrangement. That was fine with me. Afterward she kissed me several times. She stayed a few minutes and then tiptoed to the door. She had no trouble finding the door in the pitch darkness. I still could not see anything. The blurry image disappeared through the doorway and the door closed quietly.

In the morning I awoke to the smell of coffee. After washing and dressing I packed my things. Downstairs I found Mr. Metz in the dining room reading a book.

"Good morning, Mr. Gerhart."

"Good morning, sir."

"I see the fog has dissipated. You should have no trouble today finding the Gerharts in Lembach. Sabine is making breakfast. It should be ready in a few minutes. Please have a seat."

"Will Hélène be joining us for breakfast?"

"Hélène? No, she will not be home until later this morning. She works the evening shift at the hospital in Wissembourg. She departed shortly after supper last evening. Her cousin, who also works there, drives."

I took a seat across from Mr. Mertz. Thoughts were going around in my head. Sabine brought the eggs, sausage, and a baguette. When she returned to the kitchen I could not avoid noticing how her tight, satiny dress accentuated her firm and lovely-shaped ass.

Sabine joined us for breakfast. She didn't say a word. After coffee I stood while declaring it was time for me to be on my way.

"Thank you, Mrs. Metz and Mr. Metz for your hospitality. You have been very generous."

Mr. Metz stood and took hold of my briefcase.

"I'll walk you to your auto."

Sabine showed me a smile.

At the Peugeot Mr. Metz placed my suitcase in the trunk. Standing beside the vehicle, he handed me the map he had made.

"Here, I am certain you can follow my directions to Lembach. You should be there in 20 minutes time."

I slipped the paper into my pocket and moved behind the steering wheel.

"Thank you, again, Mr. Metz, for everything."

He looked at me, hesitating.

"One other thing."

"Yes?"

He paused for a time while looking me straight in the eye.

"I hope you enjoyed your stay?"

I tried to find the right words.

"More than I would have ever expected."

"I'm pleased. Have a pleasant trip. Be sure to visit us again if you are in the vicinity."

After the Metzes I drove directly to Switzerland and returned to business. I decided that perhaps on a future trip I will try again for Lembach.

Egyptian Pounds
(A creative nonfiction short story)

I exited the rear of the hotel with the intent of finding a less expensive taxi. But the view in front of me suggested I might be making a mistake. I started to think this was not a good idea. My concern was the condition of the taxis lined up here. Their condition was less than second class. Every one of these so-called taxis bore the evidence of past encounters somewhere on the streets of Cairo. Most obviously had numerous collisions. I found myself at this spot as a result of well-intended advice given to me by my local business associate, Khalid Zaki. He told me: "There is no need to pay the high prices charged by the taxi drivers at the front of the hotel. Those people have no shame. The drivers who regularly wait on the street behind the hotel will offer you much better rates. Why waste money?"

I begin to doubt that I will actually hire one of these drivers. Changing to a slower pace, I give consideration to using a taxi at the front of the hotel as I had on previous days. However, to do that I would need to re-enter the hotel and subject myself to the regular questions and searches. Are you a guest at the hotel? May I see your briefcase? I could do it if necessary, but I would rather not. As I ponder my next move, one of the drivers notices my interest, hesitant as it is, and after stamping out his cigarette, hurries over to greet me.

"In need of a ride, sir?"

The man has a large scar on his left cheek and small,

shifting eyes. I could believe he spent time in a jail somewhere for a wrong he did to someone. He has that look about him. Hesitating, and uncertain that I should hire this man, I nevertheless tell him:

"I must go to Heliopolis. You would need to wait there for about two hours and then return here."

"I will be pleased to take you. That would be 80 pounds."

Khalid was correct, I tell myself. The prices are much better here than what is available at the front of the hotel. In fact, the same service from the front of the hotel, although in a vehicle of better condition, would be more than 180 pounds. I decide that perhaps I am ready for a little adventure after all. Why waste money?

"Fine," I respond.

"My name is Hussein. Please get in. My taxi is the first in the line. You may use the other door. The one on this side does not open easily."

I walk around the car and enter from the street side. All of the other drivers momentarily stop chatting and watch me enter Hussein's taxi. I do not recognize the make of the vehicle. Perhaps it is Russian or maybe Yugoslavian. Hussein takes his seat in the front and starts the engine. My window does not go up, but that is all right. Since the air conditioner does not appear to be functioning I will need some ventilation.

Within minutes we are on the Ramses Highway. The painted lines suggest that the highway was intended to be a four-lane traffic route, but at any one point there are from four to seven vehicles abreast. "Bluffing" is the game played here on the streets. The drivers of the less battered cars do less of it; the battered vehicles, more. Hussein wins at every bluff. The outside of his vehicle suggests he yields to no man.

All vehicles come to a halt. Perhaps it is due to an accident up ahead. I could easily reach over and touch the shoulder of the driver next to us. The man glances at Hussein. Drivers try to take a measure of the competition. Forward movement resumes and Hussein is quick to advance. He pulls in front of a new Toyota and the driver of that car allows Hussein to have the advantage. Another competition won.

On the way to our destination Hussein makes no attempt at conversation, unlike most taxi drivers in Cairo. To avoid appearances of being a prig, I make a try at conversation.

"Hussein, I must say travelling in Cairo is an adventure."

"Oh, yes. Many foreigners say that. Perhaps it is because the drivers in Cairo view the task of driving in a different manner than drivers elsewhere. You see, when an Egyptian enters a car the first thing he does is to place his fate in the hands of Allah. In his heart he knows that Allah has already decided the driver's fate. Perhaps it has been decided that he is to arrive safely, but it could be otherwise too. So, the thinking is that there is no way to change fate and, furthermore, there is no need to waste time. With that understanding a driver will start the engine, take a breath, and press the accelerator to the floor."

Pedestrians have their own philosophy. On the highway I spot a man up ahead crossing the street, calmly carrying a bag of groceries. He makes no attempt to look at oncoming traffic. With no regard to the speed, direction, or attitude of the approaching vehicles, he walks on without concern. Egyptian law states it is illegal to run over pedestrians and that seems to be adequate for this man. A driver in a Jaguar heads directly for him. At first it seems the driver had failed to see him. At the last moment, the driver swerves slightly and zooms within inches of the man's back. The man neither looks left nor right, continuing to cross the highway. Perhaps he also believes in fate.

Hussein makes no more effort at conversation.

Eventually we arrive at our destination and without incident. Khalid greets me as before:

"Pleasant trip?"

"Oh, yes. An adventure every mile."

"I understand. In time you will become accustomed to people on the streets of Cairo. Most newcomers do."

After my business meeting, I return to the "taxi" where Hussein is sleeping in the front seat. He stirs when I open the rear door.

"Shall we return to the hotel now, sir?"

"Yes, please."

We do the reverse trip. Almost to the hotel, Hussein runs over a nail and the rear left tire goes flat. Hussein pulls the taxi over to the right of the road. However, Egypt is a country where good land is scarce. There is very little space off the highway. The left two wheels remain a yard onto the roadway. Hussein jacks the taxi up and fetches the spare to replace the wounded wheel. His butt extends a yard plus a little more into the travel lane. Vehicles whiz within inches of Hussein. He takes no notice. Perhaps it would be more accurate to say he appears to show no concern. The flat tire goes into the trunk and we continue to the hotel.

At the hotel Hussein pulls into the street where we had started hours earlier. He parks at the rear of the line of waiting vehicles and politely opens the rear door for me. Moving to the curb, and smiling for the first time, he tells me:

"Sir, that will be 80 pounds, British."

Obviously he is pretending that he thinks I am British and not American. We both know that ten Egyptian pounds are worth only one British pound. He is hoping to obtain a week's pay from a single trip. Now I understand why Hussein had no interest in conversation. He intended to project a tough profile.

Hesitating for effect I respond: "No, we agreed on 80 pounds, Egyptian. We are in Egypt, not Britain. I am American. Why would I agree to pay you in British money? Besides, I have no British money."

Hussein steps closer, the smile gone with a stance that appears threatening. I suspect he has used this routine many times with English-speaking tourists. It is a scheme that no doubt has brought this man extra income over the years. But I consider myself as other than a typical tourist, let alone a gullible one. Standing inches from me he tells me:

"Listen, mister. Whenever I take an English-speaking customer on a trip I always quote the price in British pounds. They understand British money better than Egyptian. You wait here. I will bring another driver over to tell you that what I say is the truth."

With that, Hussein turns and hustles over to the nearby waiting drivers. I remain in place. In a matter of minutes Hussein returns with another, much larger, man. Hussein's attempts at intimidation continue.

Hussein tells me, "This is Ashraf. He is another of our drivers out here behind the hotel."

Ashraf says, "I can tell you, sir, that for English-speaking customers most of the drivers quote rides in British pounds. It is a rate that English people understand. Hussein tells me you are American. But we cannot determine this before someone enters our taxis. And it would be impolite to ask such questions."

The charade continues. Although I feel sorry for the predicament in which these people find themselves, I greatly resent someone, poor or otherwise, trying to cheat me.

Unintimidated, I remove 80 pounds, Egyptian, from my wallet and in one motion slap the large bills on the hood while giving Hussein a steady look in the eye. I do not look at the second intimidator. No tip today!

"There," I tell him.

With that I turn and walk toward the rear entrance of the hotel. I hear nothing more from behind.

For my next trip, I will go to the front of the hotel.

Too-late Dowry
(A fictional short story)

Shankar Bhattacharya had requested the day off from work at the tannery. He told his supervisor the day would be his fifth wedding anniversary and he hoped to spend the day with his wife.

The day of the anniversary Shankar slept until midday. When he awoke he decided not to bother shaving or washing. In the kitchen, his wife, Rena, had bread on the table and water on the stove for tea. As he entered the kitchen he glanced at his wife but said nothing.

"Cheer up, Shankar."

She had decided she would not be the first to mention the "anniversary" word.

Shankar and Rena lived in a small two room flat in a poor section of Mumbai. The building always smelled of a hundred different meals and the stairwells were mostly littered with trash that the residents expected others to retrieve. Since their rooms were on the uppermost floor many days the sun would beat down on the roof, half baking the unfortunates who lived below. In winter there was no heating and room temperatures sometimes fell to near freezing. The flat was the best they could afford. The other occupants of the building were similar people. Everyone was struggling to merely stay alive. Few in the building had hopes of moving to better quarters anytime soon.

Rena added to her efforts.

"Tell you what. I am going to make your favorite dish tonight. Yesterday I bought some chickpeas, yogurt and an eggplant."

With a side glance and a sly smile, she added, "I have another surprise, but I am not telling you just yet."

Rena was a plain looking woman. She was slender and lacking the curves men preferred to see on a woman. Her appearance no doubt played a part in her eventual need to marry below her caste. She was adamant that she did not wish to grow old alone. It was for this reason her father felt obliged to offer a dowry that was more than a token. Despite circumstances she continually displayed a cheerful disposition. Everyone said she was congenial and pleasant. Rena tried her best to keep her husband happy despite his moods and his rough ways. She often thought that if she could only have a baby. How wonderful that would be. A child, preferably a boy, would give Shankar an improved attitude. But after five years there was no baby and hope that one might come along was slipping away. The absence of children was a great disappointment since the relatives on both sides were in the custom of having large families.

Finishing the tea, Shankar remained unsmiling and quiet. He ignored Rena's attempts to humor him. Rising from the table he walked to the closet and withdrew the only jacket he owned. Slipping an arm into a sleeve, he turned to Rena.

"Yes, I know it is our anniversary. It was five years ago today. I am sure you remember. That was the day your father reaffirmed the promise of a dowry. The dowry that has yet to be delivered."

"Shankar, we have discussed the dowry many times? Father is a man of his word and he will deliver the dowry exactly as he promised. Recent years have been difficult for him. He has three more daughters to marry off. And, business at his shop has declined because of increased competition. I am certain he will keep his promise as soon as he can possibly do so. There is no question of that."

Shankar turned and walked toward the door. Over his shoulder he said he was going to visit Samir. After he closed the door, Rena engaged the deadbolt. In this neighborhood one needed be ever cautious. She walked slowly to the kitchen table and sat. Her hands began to shake. She dropped her head to her hands and began to sob softly.

Outside Shankar found it was raining lightly. It was pre-monsoon weather and in the coming weeks the rains would be unceasing day after day. He decides to walk the distance regardless of the weather and without an umbrella.

Arriving at Samir's apartment, Samir's wife met him at the door.

"Oh, Shankar, come in. Let me take your coat. How are you? We have not seen you for some time. I presume you wish to see your brother."

"If he is up and about. How is he doing? Better, I hope."

Shanta looked down at her brother-in-law's feet. His shoes and clothing were soaking wet but she said nothing. She was not especially fond of this particular in-law. Mostly she resented the way the man treated his wife. Also, he always smelled of the tannery and cow hides. She guessed that he bathed only infrequently. On every family occasion she was polite to him but rarely had she gone beyond politeness.

"Your brother is still a little shaky on his feet but he will be glad to see you. He's growing tired of being house-bound and not being able to walk about. Right now he's in the kitchen, reading."

Samir and Shanta lived in a three room apartment that had a bathroom, hot water and heat. The place was luxurious compared to Shankar's quarters. Samir had always been imaginative at finding ways to make money.

In the kitchen, Samir was obviously happy to see his younger brother.

"Have a seat. Good to see you."

"I suspected you would be home what with the foot problem. How is it?"

"Improving. Every day I'm a little better. I believe I will be able to return to the store next week."

Samir was manager of a small clothing store, but he had other sources of income. He was resourceful and imaginative. He was good at reasoning things through. That was why Shankar often looked to him for advice.

"How is it going with you and Rena?

Shankar hesitated while looking at his hands.

"I'm not so sure. Today is our fifth anniversary."

"Yes. I almost forgot. Congratulations."

"Thank you."

Noise in one of the bedrooms was followed by the sound of running, small feet. Samir's three year old boy appeared and explained to his father that his bear lost a leg. Shankar's heart fell at the sight of his nephew. The boy reminded him of what he missed in life.

"Dipak, don't worry. Your mother will sew the leg on. Your bear will be as good as new. Maybe better. Give the bear to your mother. I am visiting with your uncle Shankar. Now run along."

Shanta heard the commotion and appeared with a towel and sandals for Samir. She placed the towel on a chair in front of Shankar and the sandals on the floor near his wet feet. She forced a smile for Shankar's benefit.

"I thought you might be able to use these."

Bending down she took hold of her son and retreated to one of the bedrooms. After she had closed the bedroom door, Shankar faced his brother.

"You are lucky, Samir, to have two lovely little boys. I envy you."

"They are great boys, especially the older one. He's as sharp as a tack."

Samir started to say more about the children but then stopped. He remembered children were a sore subject with his brother. He did not wish to be seen as talking excessively about children.

"I know you and Rena would like to have children. It's not too late. You still have time."

"I appreciate your good wishes, but, no, I suspect I am married to a dry cow."

"Oh, I don't know. Children are a wonderful addition to the family but they are not everything. You have a good wife. She cares a lot for you and she is the best cook of the whole relationship. Besides, marrying a wife who is a caste higher never hurts a man in India. It often leads to better things. In my opinion you made a good marriage."

"I'm glad you think so. Of course, it's easy for you to say. You have what I call a beautiful apartment. You have children. And, you actually received the promised dowry. I find myself in very different circumstances."

"Don't dwell on the dowry. You will drive yourself crazy. How about your father-in-law finding you steady employment with one of his business contacts? That was certainly worth something. In a way that favor was better than a dowry. As you are no doubt aware many of our relatives live in filth and many days have nothing to eat. Here is more food for thought. Right now you are king of the roost. Rena treats you like royalty. She waits on you day and night. Cooks whatever you choose. If there were children that arrangement would surely change. Being a mother realigns a woman's priorities. It's human nature. What I am saying is that you cannot have everything in reality exactly the way you find them in your dreams. Besides, if she hasn't become pregnant it could be your fault. It is not always the woman's fault you know."

"The work that Mr. Dutt found for me was only for the reason that he wanted to be sure his daughter would have food and shelter on a regular basis. As far as her not becoming pregnant, well, that must be her fault."

Neither man spoke. Momentarily Shanta returned to the kitchen. In time she delivered up a tray with a pot of tea, cups and a plate of biscuits. She looked at Shankar.

"The biscuits are a day old but this kind seem to age well. I think you will like them anyway."

She turned and exited without another word.

Samir poured the tea and gestured toward the biscuits.

"Help yourself."

"Thank you. I might have a biscuit at that."

Shankar took a bite from a biscuit and followed it with a sip of tea. Returning the tea cup to the saucer he faced Samir. He had become pensive.

"There's a fellow at the tannery by the name of Abhi Banerjee. We got to know one another fairly well. Abhi lives a block from us. The building where he lives is worse than the one where we live if you can believe that. They have one boy. He was not paid his promised dowry after three years. He became so upset and angry ..."

Anticipating his brother's trend of thought Samir interrupts.

"That's enough. You should not be thinking along those lines. That would be entirely uncalled for. I understand what is eating at you. The dowry. The lack of children. These things are not everything in life. Far from it. You should understand that.

Besides, you might be paid the dowry someday. And children could still come along. All of these things are still possible. Think of it that way. When all is said and done you may not be able to find a better wife. You would be out of employment for a long time. And, you might also find yourself in serious trouble with the law."

Shankar was not hearing the kind of advice that he had anticipated. There was no affirmation of his reasoning. Silent, he took another sip of tea.

"It is something I have been considering for some time. I really become angry when I think of the way I have been cheated. Really, I don't think there would be any trouble. The police usually do not concern themselves with these happenings. These events are common occurrences."

"Brother, you are talking about dangerous and unnecessary steps. I suspect the reason for your visit is to seek my opinion. My advice is that you should behave yourself. Forget the dowry for now. Personally, I would like to see you find contentment with your present wife. Furthermore, I would not like to see you spend a part of your life sitting in a prison cell."

Shankar did not touch the towel or the sandals. He knew he would be walking again in rain on the return trip to his flat. In addition, he preferred to avoid being indebted to Shanta for the slightest favor. The brothers continued talking for a spell but only innocuous topics were bandied about. When the tea was gone Shankar announced he must be going. As he stood, he wished his brother well. Samir looked up from his chair.

"You should visit us more frequently. Bring Rena next time.

At the door, Shanta handed him his jacket but, because it was still raining, he merely threw it over his arm. They both tried to be outwardly pleasant to one another.

"The tea and biscuits were very good. I would have sworn you had made the biscuits today."

"Glad you liked them. Come more often, Shankar."

In the street the rain had increased. Shankar was the only person in sight without an umbrella. On the way home he walked through the puddles rather than around them. He was in deep thought.

At the flat Shankar tapped on the front door and Rena pulled it open.

"Welcome home traveler."

Shankar walked through the door, dripping water.

"My word, you are soaking wet. I'll find you some dry clothes. Come in the bedroom."

Rena retrieved dry clothing and placed it on the bed. A moment later she returned with a large towel.

"I must look after some things cooking on the stove."

Rena returned to the kitchen to check on her dishes. Meanwhile Shankar used the towel to dry himself and then dressed with the dry clothing. His jaw was set as he walked into the kitchen. Standing behind Rena he spotted a heavy cast iron skillet on the table. Rena had received it as a wedding gift. He took hold of the skillet and in one wide swing struck his wife of five years a vicious blow. The wife who could not conceive. The wife whose father did not deliver on his promise of a dowry. As her body lay on the floor Shankar took a seat at the kitchen table and began to weep. He felt hopeless. For the next hour he paced back and forth in the small flat, telling himself he did what was necessary. He reasoned his taking action was demanded by the situation. Eventually he walked to the police station and reported that his wife had an accident in the kitchen. He said it seemed she fell and hit her head. She was unresponsive.

Two policemen returned with Shankar to the flat. After inspecting the body one policeman looked at the other. Before he could speak Shankar said he must use the toilet down the hall. As he walked toward the door he added that he will return in a few minutes. When he was out the door each policeman took half of the rupees that had been placed on the kitchen table. When Shankar returned the senior policeman explained his interpretation.

"Looks as though she slipped on some cooking oil that had spilled on the floor. Apparently she hit her head as she fell. We see this kind of accident frequently. You would think women would be more careful. If you like we will notify her family."

"Would you, please? I am a little distraught at the present. Her parents live in the fifth block of Hill Street. They own a clothing store there called "Bargain Clothing." Their apartment is on the second floor above the shop."

The policemen walked directly to the clothing shop and rang the apartment bell. In time Mrs. Banerjee opened the door. She was shocked to see policemen standing there in rain slickers.

"Oh, my word. Is something wrong, officers?"

"Sorry, mam. Are you Mrs. Banerjee?

"Yes, I am Mrs. Banerjee."

"We would like to speak with Mr. Banerjee if he is home."

"I am sorry. He is not here at the moment."

"Do you know when he will return?"

"Shortly, I presume. Today is my one daughter's wedding anniversary. My husband said he was going to deliver a dowry to my daughter's husband. First he was going to stop at the bank. Perhaps he will stay for a brief celebration. I am uncertain."

Mrs. Banerjee's comments confirmed what the policemen had surmised.

"Sorry to bother you, Mrs. Banerjee. We will return later in the day to speak with Mr. Banerjee."

It was their practice to address only the man of the house with matters Of importance.

Jim and the Big Black Skunk
(A creative nonfiction short story)

I don't trap anymore. One reason is that I live in a city and far from where a worthwhile number of furbearers may be found. But, I enjoy reading trapping stories. And, I enjoy recalling memories of those days when I went afield with traps in hand and hopes of bringing home furbearers.

I began trapping at about the age of ten. That was at a time when pelt prices made the effort well worthwhile. Trapping seemed like an easy way of making money when compared to alternatives. In the summer I could make a little pocket money cutting Mrs. Reeser's lawn. At that age, Mrs. Reeser's lawn looked to me to be about the size of a Kansas wheat field. And, using a push-em lawn mower often required that I back up to get a running start at the grass. But I had the perseverance and I wanted the money, so I did it. And, often! During the winter, trapping represented the other big money-making opportunity. Then skunk or muskrat pelts would bring real money. Besides, I loved being out in the woods alone with my dog and my trusty single shot .22 rifle. Anything that brought me outdoors was a good thing, especially if there was some pocket money to be made. So, trapping became an easy decision.

At the time, our family lived outside a small town by the name of Perrysville that is was about fifteen miles north of Pittsburgh, Pennsylvania. Nearby there were old farms and forested hills with ample game and some furbearers. In particular, there was an abundant supply of skunks, opossums, raccoons, a few weasels and muskrats. Skunks were very popular then and on Sundays women were proud to wear their skunk coats. I always thought skunk pelts made a fine garment. Few furs had the shine and luster of skunk. With time, however, the popularity of skunk coats waned due to a slight lingering scent the coat makers could not seem to eliminate.

About my second year of trapping a friend of mine, Jim Faust, also took up trapping. Jim and I had much in common and we would often get together to go hunting or trapping. We went to the same school in Perrysville and we often had opportunities to compare notes. Jim trapped exclusively on the west side of Route 19 which ran through the center of Perrysville, and I trapped only on the east side. Anyhow, one year we decided it would be a good idea to form a partnership to do our trapping. We thought that if one of us wanted to take a day off, the other partner would then tend to both traplines. It would be a different approach to trapping as we had been practicing it, and we agreed to try it for a while. We did the partnership arrangement for a few weeks, but eventually decided it would be best if we each returned to tending our own traps.

While we were still partners, Jim told me one day that the owner of the Perrysville bakery asked him if he might be interested in trapping some skunks. The bakery building was on stilts and it was easy for people or animals to walk under the rear part of the building. Some skunks seemed to especially like the building design. The skunks had dug a den underneath the building and it seemed several were living there. This created a slight problem for the baker. Some days, above the smell of baked bread, a slight smell of skunk could be detected. Little did the baker know! Jim and I thought, "What the heck"–another skunk pelt would be the equivalent of a few more bucks in the piggy bank. The bakery was on the east side of Route 19, and Jim said he would take care of the bakery skunks.

Whenever we were making sets for skunks, Jim and I used an arrangement of our own design. We would use a stick of about six feet in length. The trap chain would be secured to one end of the stick. The other end would be tied to a tree or a stake. Whenever we found a skunk in the trap, this arrangement would allow us to unfasten the end opposite the skunk and then slowly lift the skunk up in the air. We would always work in slow motion so as to avoid frightening the skunk. Once off the ground, a skunk will not use his perfume defense. Then the skunk would be taken for a swim in the local stream. This way the skunk would not release his potent defense and usually there was very little resulting odor. This was a procedure that both Jim and I had used numerous times and it had always worked well for us.

Well, the first night Jim had a hit under the bakery. It was a large, totally black skunk which was considered the best of all kinds. The less white, the better the price. So, Jim at first was delighted. However, there was a slight problem. Jim explained the baker had stored a number of boards under the building and most were in an upright position. The skunk had entangled the trap chain around the base of several of these vertical boards. Jim's first feelings of delight were about to turn into other types of feelings! Jim told me he had to get down on all fours in an effort to untangle the trap chain. This required that he come closer than desired to the trapped animal. Anyhow, Jim said he decided to try to gently untangle blackie from the troublesome boards while, at the same time, on all fours.

Jim said all was going well until his foot struck one of the upright boards which then tilted over and fell on the skunk. That did it! From a distance of about four feet, the startled skunk did a quick 180 and let Jim have it full force.

It was a chilly November day, but when Jim arrived home his mother would initially not allow him in the house. The smell was that strong! Jim was handed a shovel and told to bury his clothes in the garden. Returning in his underwear, he was finally allowed in his house.

Jim and I went to the same schoolroom although he was one class ahead of me. Each classroom had two classes and one teacher. Every other year we would be in the same classroom. That year we were in the same classroom. Each of the classes consisted of about a dozen students but there were a number of empty seats in the rear of the room. So, the teacher made Jim sit as far back in the classroom as possible. There, he was all by himself and about ten feet from the nearest student. His normal friends avoided him to the maximum extent possible.

The owner of the Perrysville Bakery was royally upset. Whereas he had though there was a mild problem due to the slight skunk odor, he now realized he had a much larger problem. Regular customers would come to the front door, open it, take a whiff and do a quick turnaround. I suspect that the bakery's bottom line was a little less than normal for a month or so. I understand that the baker stopped talking to members of the Faust family. Our family didn't buy our bread there, so we had no problem. Eventually, Jim's odor of skunk went away, and the usual customers returned to the bakery. So, the damage was only temporary.

I often think of Jim and the great outdoor adventures we had those days in Perrysville. To this day I am glad it was not my turn to visit the traps under the bakery.

A Family Affair
(A fictional short story)

Masoud decided it was time to exit the café and return home. He had grown tired of smoking the water pipe. Besides, his mother would soon have lunch ready. Approaching the house where he lived, he spotted his father standing outside the front door. His father was always serious but this day his demeanor was both serious and sad as well. Masoud immediately knew that there was something drastically wrong. When Masoud came closer, his father whispered, "Your sister was raped."

The message was clear and immediately understood. There was no need for additional words. Both father and son realized it was an unfortunate mistake on her part. She should have been more careful. The responsibility fell to Masoud, the eldest of the two sons. He told his father, "I will do what is necessary."

The father added, "Be certain to avoid disruptive acts within someone's home. That would be unacceptable."

The father lowered his gaze. Dejected, he slowly entered his house.

Masoud climbed the stairs to the second floor and the bedroom he shared with his brother. He went directly to the chest of drawers and began rummaging through the clothing. First he opened the bottom drawer and then the two higher ones. He looked over at his brother who was watching television.

"Where is my khanjar? Did you see it?"

"Yes, it is there in the bottom drawer. I saw it the other day. Look again."

Masoud returned to the bottom drawer and, disturbed, grabbed all of the drawer's clothing in his arms. He threw it all on the nearest bed. There in the rear corner of the drawer he saw the khanjar, the traditional Arab knife with the curved and double edged blade. An effective implement for stabbing or slashing. It is customarily intended for special occasions and today there will be one. Withdrawn from its sheath, its suitability was confirmed. Yes, it has kept its edges and it was ready for service. The younger brother became curious about Masoud's strange and agitated behavior. He asked, "What are you doing? You expect me to put all of that stuff back?" Masoud did not respond and walked to the head of the stairs.

At the bottom of the stairs Masoud's mother was waiting for him. She suspected her son's intentions.

"Masoud I want you to come to the dining room. I will bring you some goat cheese and bread. We must talk. I will have a good lunch ready a little later. Today we are having mutton and rice."

"No, mother. I have things I must do."

"Masoud, your sister Sidra is a good girl. I don't want you concerning yourself with her."

"Where is Sidra?"

"I sent her for some desert. She will be returning shortly."

Masoud became suspicious. He was aware that mother's will protect their daughters despite the resolve of men in the family.

"I am not hungry. I don't want anything to eat now. Maybe later. Save some mutton for me."

Masoud exited the house, his khanjar well hidden beneath his outer clothing. Both he and his mother knew he would be going to the Al Hadid Road. It is the most direct route to the small town of Gigam where most of the family's relatives live. There Sidra may hope to find refuge with one of them. Perhaps she expects to find a sympathetic widow. As the door closed, Masoud's mother put her hand to her mouth. Quietly she began sobbing.

In the street Masoud wrapped his fingers around the knife's handle. It felt firm, sturdy. He had never used the weapon before. This day will bring new experiences, ones he can relate to whomever might inquire. He told himself he will be admired for his steadfastness. His family's honor will remain unsoiled.

On the Al Hadid Road, Sidra was walking as fast as she could. But she had departed in haste forgetting to change out of sandals. She had to stop constantly to remove stones and the soles of her feet were becoming bloody. It was midday and the sun was unforgiving. She had to slow her pace. Sidra began to believe she might be safe after all. Ahead she could see the house of her aunt. And the aunt was out of the house, standing near the road with folder arms. Sidra's mother must have telephoned.

The hot weather was slowing Masoud as well. But he could still make better time than his sister. He would jog for 100 meters and then slow to a walk for another 100 meters. Far ahead he, too, could see his aunt's home. He knew the house well. When he and Sidra were youngsters they had spent many hours in that house. There were many people in the streets, some going north and others the opposite direction. Ahead, he spotted a young woman in a blue dress. He knew it could be Sidra. She has few dresses and one is the same color of blue. The woman is also not wearing her usual headscarf. The slut! It will be easy to overtake her now. Yes, the knife is ready for the occasion. Frightened, Sidra turns now and then to watch behind her. She spots her brother who is now running toward her. She screams and turns to run toward the aunt. People in the street turn to look in her direction. One sandal goes free but she continues running as best as she can.

Masoud expects his sister will plead and beg but his plans have already been made. His hand grasps the knife and removes it from its sheath. It must be quick. Bystanders will watch but nobody will interfere. They will understand this is a family matter.

A Subtle Play
(A creative nonfiction short story)

Sitting in front of his computer, Eric Schuler started to nod. The afternoon was passing too slowly. He decided the situation warranted caffeine, perhaps much caffeine. In the lunch room he found the coffee pot that had been left empty by the last person to use it. He filled the coffee machine with water and, opening drawers, began searching for a fresh packet of coffee. Another development engineer, Mason Warner, who was also in need of coffee, came into the room. The two engineers had worked on several projects together and were well acquainted.

Eric was the younger of the two. He had graduated from engineering school five years ago. Eric was slender and of medium build. Although reserved in demeanor he was tough underneath. He kept in good physical condition by visiting a gym regularly and running several times a week. At Bricksen Hydraulics, Inc. he looked up to Mason much as he would to an older, wise brother.

Mason was older than Eric, a family man with a wife, a mortgage and grown children. He enjoyed beer as well as eating, and his profile showed it. Mason often took time to educate Eric on the company's product line. He pointed to the cabinets over the coffee machine.

"The coffee is up there. Pam moved it there the other day."

Eric retrieved a packet and emptied it into the machine.

"It'll be few minutes, but I'm waiting. I'm in need of a jolt.

The stuff I'm doing is boring, although it does seem necessary. The late night party didn't help matters. For sure I don't want to be caught napping like Warren Beaton."

"What do you mean? What happened to Warren? I noticed he hasn't been at work for a day or two."

"You didn't know? Levan caught him sleeping in front of his computer. Shook him by the shoulder and gave him an ass-chewing. Told him to go home and do his sleeping there. He's making him take a week off without pay."

"No, I didn't hear about that. As you might have noticed by now, people don't talk to one another much around here. Nobody wants to be accused of gossiping on company time."

Both watched the level slowly rise in the coffee pot. When the dripping stopped, each poured a cupful and sat at the nearest table. After taking a sip Mason looked at Eric.

"How long have you been with the company?"

"A little more than two years. How about you?"

"Me? Eleven years—eleven long years. I would have liked to go elsewhere but I couldn't. I had kids in school and now my wife has a good job in town. Moving would cause too much financial pain."

Chuck Longenecker, one of the designers, entered the lunch room and went directly to the coffee pot.

Eric took a sip of the hot coffee.

"Ah, I needed that."

Both sat in silence and watched Chuck look for a cup. Eric caught Mason's eye.

"You've been here long enough to know Paul Levan. Does he ever say good morning?"

Mason turned to see if Chuck was watching and then raised a finger to his lips. Eric had started to say more but stopped short. Chuck Longenecker poured his coffee and headed for the door, turning to see who had been speaking. Together, Eric and

Mason rose and in silence walked to Eric's cubicle. Mason finished his coffee and threw the empty Styrofoam cup in Eric's wastebasket. He turned to Eric.

"Have you found a girlfriend since you've been in town?"

"Yes, Pam gave me a number of a niece and I called her. She's a school teacher by the name of Gina. We've been on two dates. She's a pleasant and interesting girl but nothing serious."

"If you are not doing anything Saturday evening why don't you and Gina come over to the house? I'll throw something on the grill. You can meet my wife. She's from Pittsburgh too. You two can talk about rusting steel mills. We'll have a few beers and play some cards. I'll assume you like bratwursts and baked potatoes."

"Thank you. That would be great. What time?"

"Say around seven."

***

Saturday evening Eric and Gina appeared at the front door of 3328 Cindy Drive. Eric knocked and shortly Mason appeared.

"Welcome. I suggest you walk around the house to the backyard. That way you won't break any bones tripping on live animals."

Behind the house Mason's wife, Maxine, was in a lounge chair reading a paperback. Introductions were made. Mason handed a bottle of Pinot Noir to Mason.

"Here's something to go with the meal. I don't know though. Does red wine go with bratwurst and potatoes?"

Mason shrugged.

"I wouldn't know. I'm from Milwaukee. We don't drink wine in Milwaukee. It could lead to mass unemployment. Just kidding. We'll try the wine later and find out. Right now we have a case of Milwaukee Miller dark at the ready."

Maxine approached Gina.

"Are you from Ft. Wayne, Gina?"

"Yes, I'm sorry to say. Are you?"

"No, I'm from Pittsburgh much like Eric."

"Oh, Eric often talks about Pittsburgh. The hills and the rivers, but no I've never been there. I know nothing about Pittsburgh."

"Some people say Pittsburgh is a good city to be from. Would you like a beer or perhaps a mixed drink."

"No, thank you. Maybe later. By the way, I like your beveled glass front door. Very different. You don't see doors like that in the newer houses."

"Thank you. I'm glad you liked it. We bought it at an antique dealer a few years ago. Mason installed it himself. Come on, I'll show you the house while the guys are tending the grill."

The two women walked toward the house, chatting. When they opened the rear door a cat streaked around their legs into the back yard. The men brought bratwurst and potatoes to the grill. Mason lit the grill and placed the food above a low flame.

"That's going to take an hour or so. How about a beer in the meantime?"

"Sure."

"Be right back."

Mason returned with two bottle of Miller's dark and handed one to Eric.

"There are more where these came from."

"Dark. You like the dark?"

"It's an old Milwaukee tradition this time of the year. It has something to do with the breweries cleaning the vats in the springtime. I like this one because it has a good punch to it and not because it's dark."

"I don't remember drinking any dark beers before."

"You would if you were from a beer town. Listen, Eric. I would like to tell you something. You're a likeable guy. In a way you remind me of a younger me. Except that you are smarter.

We both moved to this little town to take a job offered by Paul Levan."

"Do I detect regrets?"

"Yes and no. The job puts food on the table. No complaints there. As long as I do my work, keep my head low and my mouth shut I will probably be able to keep my job until retirement. But, if I were younger like you I would be gone in a flash. This Levan guy is hard to deal with. I've become good at biting my tongue. In fact I'm expert at it."

"Does that have anything to do with your raising a finger to your lips the other day in the lunch room? I was merely going to asking if Levan was in the practice of saying good morning or not saying good morning. I walked by him several times since I've been here and I always said 'good morning' but every time he simply ignored me. As far as I am concerned, it's no big deal one way or the other. It's merely that I thought it seemed strange. He was more than congenial when I came for the interview. In fact he invited me to his house for drinks that evening. I met his wife and we all talked for a while."

"There are some things you need to understand. Paul Levan does not like anything other than praise and admiration. It's part of his plan to remain as head of engineering department well into the foreseeable future. And, you need to know that he has a network of spies to help ensure he remains number one. The rumor is that he rewards his informers well. Some of them, incompetence aside, have kept their jobs because they are willing to rat on their unsuspecting coworkers. That designer, Longenecker, who came into the lunch room the other day when we were talking, is said to be one of the spies. From what I can tell, that is most likely a true rumor. It's hard to tell for sure who the others might be."

"Strange."

"Some of the stories are hard to believe. There was a

designer a few years ago who went into Levan's office to ask for a raise. He said he hadn't had a raise in seven years. I knew the guy. He was a hard worker and good at what he did. Levan thought he, chief engineer, should be the one to not only decide who gets a raise but when and how much. He did not care to have underlings challenging his generosity. To make an example of the guy he had him transferred to quality control where his hourly rate was decreased by five dollars. The man did the job for a month and then quit the company."

The brats started to drip fat onto the flames and smoke began to rise from the grill. Mason walked over to turn the brats and potatoes. Satisfied that all is well at the grill, he went inside the house and shortly returned with two more cold beers. He handed one to Eric.

"Drink up."

"Thanks. These dark ones are filling."

"Inside I have some ale. We'll switch to those next. Before the sausages are ready and we go inside, there is something else I wanted to tell you. I saw your resume before you came with the company. Levan often sends resumes around before he hires someone. I don't know why. Anyway, I could see you have a promising future. But, I must tell you, probably not at Bricksen Hydraulics. I'll tell you why. Levan has been pressured to hire promising engineers, engineers like yourself. The sales department has been pressing hard for product improvements and new products. The salesmen keep saying our line of actuators is behind the times and in need of upgrades. Levan said he would look for new talent, but it is all a show. He personally designed many of the company's products in years gone by. Those products have Levan's name associated with them. It appears he is encouraging progress and product improvements but in actuality he's been a major impediment. After a new engineer acquires experience, Levan finds an excuse to get rid of him. I've seen it happen and you, personally, can expect no different treatment. He intends to keep Paul Levan's light shining the brightest. Screw the company's bottom line."

"Interesting. I appreciate the insight."

When the brats and potatoes were ready, Eric and Mason went inside where the women were waiting. Maxine had placed salads on the table. The Pinot Noir was opened and each had a glass with the meal. After desert Mason fetched two ales from the refrigerator and handed one to Eric.

"Oh, I don't know about another beer."

"Why not?"

"Don't you know 'Bier auf Wein das lass' sein aber Wine auf Bier das rat' ich dir?' "

"No. what's that mean?"

"My grandfather told me that. It's an old German saying that means one should not drink beer after wine but that drinking wine after beer is ok."

"You would be at home in Milwaukee. You only had one glass of wine. You'll be ok."

"I'll try it. At the worst I'll only get sick."

After supper they played Texas hold 'em for pennies. The men continued with the ale while the women drank sodas. At 1:00 a.m. Eric declared it was time to go. Standing, he thanked Mason and Maxine for the evening. While driving Gina home Eric was quiet and pensive. He was trying to put Mason's comments about Chief Engineer Levan into perspective. Maybe formulate a plan. He started feeling nauseous.

***

Monday morning Eric was early to the office. By 9:30 o'clock he figured he was eligible for a break and walked to Mason's cubicle. He tapped on the frame of the entrance.

"Ready for a break?"

Mason placed his computer in sleep mode and rose.

"Good idea."

The two walked to the lunch room. Eric filled two cups and passed one to Mason.

"This one's on me."

"You're too generous."

"We enjoyed ourselves the other night. Thanks again."

"Don't mention it. Maxine and I were glad to have you over. We'll do it again sometime. That Gina's a pretty girl and smart too. She took all my pennies."

Eric said, "I gave more thought to your comments about our chief engineer. Your observations explain a lot of situations. For example, several times I made a number of recommendations for product improvements. These were no brainers. It's not as though I am a genius or anything like that. Anyone would have recognized the need. Yet, Paul always found a reason for turning them down. My career will be going nowhere if I cannot point to designs and contributions that I have made. It's the business I'm in. It's how I earn my living."

"You're starting to catch on. But, do me a favor. Please don't tell anyone I coached you. For sure that would be my end here and it might happen at an inconvenient time."

"You have my word. Of course. Listen, I've been giving thought to sending my resume out again. Perhaps the time has arrived for me to make a career change."

"Are you hoping to stay in Ft. Wayne or doesn't that matter?"

"I have no connections here, so I can go anywhere there is a good opportunity."

"You've been around the block a few times. Any suggestions as where might be a good place to start?"

"Well, I suggest you might consider our customers. Some of them might be in need of an engineer who knows hydraulics as you now do."

***

Eric came to the conclusion that, all things considered, Mason seemed to be correct in his assessments. It might be time for a move. After sending resumes to several prospective employers he received two interesting invitations for interviews. One firm, Dobson Equipment, seemed especially attractive. Dobson was a firm that had consistently placed large orders for hydraulic actuators and accessories with Bricksen Hydraulics. Gradually he began to wonder why he waited so long to consider leaving Bricksen and its corrupt engineering department.

Eric's interview at Dobson went well. The chief engineer told Eric that Dobson was considering him for a role in the selection and application of hydraulic components. The following week Eric received an offer of employment that included what would be a sizable pay increase. The following week he called the chief engineer at Dobson and they agreed on a starting date three weeks in the future. Eric said he would like to take a vacation of two weeks and then another week to find an apartment and move. The chief engineer at Dobson said that would be fine and that he looked forward to having Eric on his team of engineers.

***

As often happened on Monday mornings, Eric and Mason met for a coffee break. They were sitting in the lunch room when Chuck Longenecker came in for his coffee. Actually, they were expecting Chuck. Eric was sitting with his back to Chuck and the coffee machine. As Chuck was pouring coffee into a cup, Eric starting talking to Mason.

"As I mentioned, I could not believe what happened. That son of a bitch Levan turned down my suggestion for changing the seals on the Model X600 actuators. Just because he selected the seals ten years ago does not make it the best today. Boy, he can be hard-headed."

Mason was careful to avoid saying anything derogatory about Chief Engineer Levan. Yet, he felt obliged to respond one way or the comments by his friend.

"Are you sure that Paul designed that sealing configuration?"

"That's what I was told by designers who were here ten years ago."

Chuck took interest in the conversation that he was overhearing. In order to remain within earshot he pretended to look for something in the drawers near the coffee machine while shuffling objects back and forth. Eventually he felt obliged to exit the lunch room.

Mid-afternoon Paul Levan had his secretary tell Eric he was wanted in Levan's office. When Eric approached the chief engineer's office he found the door open. Nevertheless, he knocked on the open door. Levan answered immediately without looking up from the letter he was reading.

"Come in."

Levan walked to a point in front of Levan's large oak desk and stood, waiting. Paul continued reading a letter without looking at Eric. In time he spoke without looking up from the letter.

"Close the door."

Eric walked over and closed the door. Neither man said a word for a time. Eventually Levan placed the letter on the corner of his desk. Without looking at Eric he told him to have a seat.

"Eric, how long have you been with us?"

"A little more than two years, sir."

"I'll be frank with you. We liked your resume when you applied for employment with us, and we thought at the time that you could bring fresh ideas to our firm. We considered you an engineer with potential. As you might be aware by now the company is very much in need of product updates and new ideas. However, you have not been of any worthwhile assistance to us to reach that end. I am obliged to bring your employment with the firm to an end. Today will be your last day with us. You have two weeks' vacation coming so we will officially consider your last day as two weeks from today. We will send you a check at the end of the month."

Eric looked dejected.

"I'm sorry you look at it that way, sir. I tried my best."

"You can clean out your desk today and go home whenever you are ready. An hour should be adequate time."

"Yes, sir."

Eric had nothing worth taking in his desk so he put on his jacket and exited through the front door.

***

Two months after Paul Levan fired Eric, Bob Ransome, General Sales Manager, walked with heavy steps to Paul Levan's office. Evelyn, Paul's secretary, was doing her nails, but she put her tools away when Bob approached.

"Mr. Levan is talking with someone at the present."

Bob continued on his path.

"I don't care."

He opened the door and walked into Paul's office. Paul and Chuck Longenecker were talking. Paul was startled since few people would walk through his door without an appointment or without knocking first. Bob pointed a finger at Paul.

"Remember that engineer Eric Whitfield that you canned some time ago?"

"What about him?"

"He's now selecting hydraulic components for Dobson Equipment, one of our biggest customers. Our salesman who calls on Dobson, Jim Gribbins, called me a few minutes ago to give me the good news."

Paul Levan stood.

"Interesting! I hadn't heard that. Why worry? I don't see a problem."

"Paul, tell me something. How in the hell are we supposed to sell our products to guys who were fired from here? In addition, I understand he didn't like our line of hydraulics while he was here. He was continually suggesting improvements—I was told. Some, I also heard, were good ideas. I hope you had a reason for letting him go."

"Bob, I'll take care of what I am paid to do, and I'm sure you will take care of selling what you are paid to sell. As far as Eric is concerned, well, he was not coming up with any good ideas while soaking up a good salary. I figured we had better ways to spend the firm's money. It's not the big deal you seem to imagine it is."

Bob Ransome pivoted on his left foot and briskly exited Paul's office without another word. After returning to his office he called the president's secretary and asked for an appointment. He added it concerned the company's chief engineer.

***

All things considered, Eric was pleased he had pulled up stakes in Ft. Wayne and moved to a strange city. Packing and engaging a mover was a chore. He said good-by to his small circle of friends. They wished him well. He had one last date with Gina. They both agreed they enjoyed each other's company. Long ago Eric decided having a good paycheck and interesting employment came first. The other amenities as friends will naturally follow.

Eric found the atmosphere at Dobson Equipment different from what he had experienced at Bricksen. New ideas were encouraged and there was a team spirit. The firm's continually increasing sales seemed to suggest a successful game plan. Five weeks after joining Dobson, Eric was at his desk reviewing the drawings of a prospective new hydraulic actuator configuration when the receptionist called.

"Eric, there is a salesman here by the name of Jim Gribbins. He says he is with Bricksen Hydraulics, and he said he would like meet with you if you are available."

It was a visit Eric expected as he knew Dobson regularly bought hydraulic components from Bricksen.

"Tell Mr. Gribbins I will be out in a few minutes."

When Eric entered the lobby, Jim Gribbins stood and extended his hand.

"Eric, I'm Jim Gribbins and I am with Bricksen. Our sales manager, Bob Ransome, called me to tell me you had joined Dobson Equipment. I just wanted to stop by and introduce myself."

The two men shook hands. Eric invited Jim to his cubicle. After they were seated Jim was the first to speak.

"I'm sure you will like it here. This is a great outfit. I've been calling on Dobson for over ten years. Your predecessor, Bill Fegley, was a sharp engineer, and he bought tons of hydraulic equipment from us over the years. As you may know he retired a few months ago."

Eric responded, "Yes, I was told Mr. Fegley retired. I saw a number of drawings with his name on them."

"I called today merely to let you know that we at Bricksen had a good working relationship with Dobson over the years and we hope to keep it that way. We will always strive to meet your needs for hydraulic equipment."

"Well, I am pleased to hear that. Of course I will try my best to give an honest evaluation to whatever you have."

"That is all anybody would ask."

Both the salesman and the engineer were silent for a spell. The salesman was first to speak again.

"Oh, I almost forgot. The sales manager at Bricksen asked me to tell you. You no doubt remember Paul Levan? He was the chief engineer at Bricksen."

"You say 'was chief engineer'?"

"Yes, he's no longer chief engineer. The president fired him a few weeks ago. He's been replaced by one of Bricksen's engineers. You probably know him. A guy by the name of Mason Keller. I understand he has been at Bricksen for some time and knows the product line."

Eric smiled.

"Yes, I remember Mason."

Jim reached into his shirt pocket and retrieved a namecard.

"Here is my namecard. I usually stop by here at least once a month to meet with the purchasing people, but today I came in merely to make your acquaintance. If you need anything please give me a call. Maybe next time we can go to lunch?"

"Sure. I always welcome a chance to get out of the office."

Eric walked Jim to the lobby where they shook hands before Jim exited through the front door. Smiling to himself, Eric returned to his cubicle.

Cousin Paul
(A creative nonfiction short story)

I wrote to Paul, but a response was not received. The second time I enclosed adequate British postage, thinking the postage might enhance my chances. It wasn't as though I was asking for a grant or a personal visit. My mere request was for an autographed photo. A souvenir to hang on the wall. Something to elicit oh's and aah's. A "Where did you ever get that?"

One would think that, if Paul did not care to be bothered, he would have a secretary to take care his fan mail. Perhaps an elderly widow in need of income to pay the rent and put food on the table. She would sit at a desk from nine until six. Except, of course, for tea breaks. She would have pre-printed notes that read, "Paul is very busy these days with travelling and performances. Nevertheless, he is dedicated to his fans and he asked me to take care of his correspondence for a time. Thank you for your request. Enclosed is a signed photograph with Paul's compliments." A name would appear at the bottom: "Gertrude Simmons." Of course her true name would be other than Gertrude Simmons. But, alas, there was no note from a Gertrude Simmons.

It was only a few years ago that I came to realize Paul and I are related. In many ways it was coincidental. I was born in Pittsburgh, two years after my mother married my father, also a

Joseph Fleckenstein. Mother was born in Ireland at a time before Ireland was an independent country. Both the Brits and the Irish laid claim to her. When she came to America she came on a British passport that said she was "a subject of the king." Yet, the Irish said she was born in Ireland and, undoubtedly, an Irish citizen. I won't belabor the point.

Because of mother, in the American way of speaking, one could say I am "half" Irish. Yet, I consider myself 100% American. (It was for that reason, I joined the Army to fight for America.) So, if I am 100% there would be 0% for anything else. Not true? Granted, it would be fair to say at least half of my heritage is Irish.

Mother came to America, alone, when she was 19, much as the Irish girl in the movie *Brooklyn*. Mother had two uncles who were already living in Pittsburgh. Initially she stayed with one uncle, Frank Martin, and his wife. Unfortunately, Frank died a year later and mother was obliged to find other accommodations. The second uncle, Henry Martin, was a confirmed bachelor. Uncle Henry, as we called him, had fought in the British Army in the First World War. It was in France where he whiffed some mustard gas the Germans sent his way. As a result, his left arm hung limp by his side. Uncle Henry was not one to forgive and forget. He decided he did not care to mix with the people who, in the past, were trying their best to do him in. Because of our German family name he placed father in the category with his former enemy. Uncle Henry would visit mother only when father was at work. He did not care to mix with people he considered to be German.

It was true that father's heritage was German, but he certainly was not "German." Father was born in the ethnic German section of the North Side of Pittsburgh. In the same neighborhood where H.J. Heinz started jarring pickles and ketchup. True, also, father spoke only German until the age of

13. That was because German was the language in the school, the church and the neighborhood. But when the First World War started, the schools switched to English and the church started having a Sunday sermon in English.

After I joined the Army, I was sent to France to stand at the gate. In a letter mother sent to me she suggested that after I had accumulated leave time I might enjoy a visit to the relatives in County Monaghan, Ireland. She suggested I write to her brother Peter. I waited for the trees to bud and mailed a letter to Uncle Peter. He answered, saying he and his wife, Roisin, would be delighted to have me visit them. I flew over that July and stayed two weeks. Uncle Peter took off from work and spent the days showing me around. I was enthralled by the different, friendly and easy-going Irish ways. It was another world.

One Saturday, Uncle Peter took me to a Gaelic game. Gaelic is the national sport and a loose combination of soccer and rugby. A rugged sport. As cousin Macartin explained, it's "unlike that sissy English sport, soccer." Only men were at the game; there was not a woman in sight. Musicians playing bagpipes added a festive air to the occasion. Before entering the stadium most men would first urinate against the facade of the structure. Not unlike foxes marking a territory.

The day of the livestock auction Peter took me to the town square at Carrickmacross. That was where the selling and buying took place. I guessed the sellers were mostly farmers and the buyers butchers. Peter knew everyone. "Come over here," he whispered to me. I followed him to where two men were dickering over the price of a hog that was in a cart between them. In all, there were about eight men gathered around the cart. Six others were nearby watching with anticipation. Finally the seller and a buyer agreed on a price. All eight went to the nearest pub for a round or two, allowing the hog and wagon to wait in the marketplace.

A number of days Peter took me around to meet our "friends." (In Irish dialect, a "friend" is a relative.) They all appeared to be younger than Americans of the same age. There were fewer wrinkles and fewer gray hairs. That was puzzling. Perhaps it was the high and pervasive humidity or the easy-going life style.

One day Uncle Peter and I were in a bar having fish and chips for lunch. The chips were served automatically with a raw egg on top. It was assumed that anyone who ordered fish and chips would want a raw egg on top. While eating I could not avoid hearing two old timers talking at the next table. One, it seemed, had worked in a local garage in his younger days. "Oh, you worked with Sean, the red head? Isn't he the one who shot the black and tan?" The second man replied, "Yeah, he said the man came nosing around one day. He told me he quietly raised the kitchen window a little and let him have it. The body is buried up in the orchard, still wearing the uniform and all." No doubt the shooting took place during the Irish uprising many years earlier.

Mother often spoke of the "troubled times." The "troubles" started when the Brits were occupied with the Germans in the fields of France during the First World War. While many Irishmen were fighting and dying for the British Empire, a goodly number were fighting against the Empire. The rebels figured it was as good a time as any to start an uprising against their English overlords. The Irish had been waiting for an opportunity for over 300 years. Eventually the struggle led to Ireland's independence but not before extensive conflict.

According to mother, one morning she and her sisters were going to school. It was during the troubled times. She spotted a large pool of blood on the road. Since she was the eldest, she ran back to the cottage to tell her mother. Her mother called the girls into the house and told them in unmistakable terms that if anyone asked "you did not see a thing." Mother said she never learned more about the blood and she asked no questions. No doubt similar scenes were repeated many times across Ireland during those times.

When Peter took me to visit friends I made notes as to whom, exactly, I had met. If for no other reason, I knew mother would be interested in hearing about my visits and people from her youth. Almost to a person, they greeted me warmly. Invariably, beer or tea was offered. They would ask about mother. "How's your dear mother? God bless her," I often heard.

One of the relatives to whom Peter introduced me was an elderly lady by the name of Ellen Winters. At the time Mrs. Winters lived alone and in a rented house near the Lisdoonan School. The location was a mere ten-minute walk from the cottage where my mother was born. A cottage with a dirt floor. A dirt floor that partly explained why the Irish longed for independence and better times.

Mrs. Winters was a gracious woman, quiet and dignified. She told me she was born a Mohan and that she was the niece to my great-grandmother, Mary Mohan. Of course, she said, she remembered her aunt well. Mary Mohan was well known amongst the relationship in large part because she "ran away" to marry my great-grandfather. I suspected Mrs. Winters was a widow, but I chose not to ask. I did not know it at the time, but later I learned Ellen Winters was the sister to Paul McCartney's grandfather, one Owen Mohan. I still have the piece of paper on which I made notes of my conversation with Mrs. Winters.

Several years after my visit to Ireland, my Aunt Roisin wrote to me one Christmas, as was her custom, and she happened to mention an interesting rumor. It seemed one of our relatives expressed the opinion that we were related to Paul McCartney, the famous Beatle. She added that the thinking was that the connection was through my grandmother, Anne Martin, and her mother Mary Mohan. Grandmother Anne Martin was a sister to Henry Martin, the ex-British soldier who fought in the Irish Brigade. I was intrigued and I immediately set out to determine if there was, as rumored, a connection. After a number of inquiries, I was put in contact with a librarian in Monaghan City, which is in that part of Ulster over the border in Northern Ireland. The woman was very helpful and sent me a number of tax records. Those records proved to be the link.

One of the tax records that I received was for a Michael Mohan who was my great-great-grandfather and likewise the great-great grandfather to Sir Paul. Mother often spoke of the man. She told me, "He always had money. They say he was in with the English." True, or not? It was not possible to be certain, either then or today. Nonetheless, it was true that there were ample informants amongst the Irish. Sadly, some did it for the money. Perhaps others did it because they truly thought that Irish independence was not a sound idea. In any event, the family tree I was able to draw from the various records showed that Paul McCartney and I are third cousins.

I have been thinking lately! Perhaps it is time for a third letter to Sir Paul. It has been six years since the second and last letter. I will remind him again that he and I are third cousins and, if he is so inclined, a signed photo would be greatly appreciated. I will remind him, or Gertrude, that he and I are, as the Irish say, friends. I was thinking that perhaps I should remind him that, despite the name, I am not really German and certainly not the enemy. Also, perhaps I should remind him that I sent suitable postage with my last letter but have as yet to receive anything in return. I must give more thought to what I will say in the third letter. Since the first two failed to catch his attention, I should come up with something very different. Something eye catching. I'm thinking, I'm thinking.

An interview with Joseph Fleckenstein
By Streetlight editor Susan Shafarzek

The light and chafing tone of this essay was one of the things that delighted me. However, I detect a deeper aspect, having to do with identity. Can you speak a little to the issue of how finding your Irish connection might have changed your own sense of who you were?

The first few paragraphs of my story have an edge that could be described as expressing resentment or disappointment. Nevertheless, it's a pretention. When I wrote to Sir Paul I suspected there was only a slim chance that he would respond. Superstar entertainers live on a plane that is entirely different from the plane that I know. I cannot say I was disappointed, let alone angry, because there was no response to my letters. It was what I expected from the start. On the other hand, I mentioned in my letters to Paul that I had tea with his grand-aunt, a woman he no doubt never met. I also mentioned a rumor about our mutual great-great grandfather. If I were in his shoes, I would have been interested in receiving the information and perhaps appreciative. But, everyone does not think as I. In fact, few do. True too: How would he know my letters were not fraudulent.

It would be incorrect to say that I found my Irish connection much as, say, a person finds a quarter that had slipped from his fingers into high grass. The quarter never slipped from my possession. I always knew I was connected to the Irish. My mother, an immigrant from Ireland, was there to remind me of that. Furthermore, it would have been difficult for me to ignore a connection to a country that claimed me as a citizen. Much as other Americans of Irish or German descent, I could never consider myself a hyphened American. No, that would not do.

The interaction between place and situation is always of interest here at Streetlight. Can you say more about how being in Ireland affected your sense of things?
The Irish do things their unique and sometimes charming ways. Because of this inclination, I found that Ireland offered up a wide variety of situations and customs that were both different and intriguing. The list is endless. Ireland is a beautiful and enchanting country.

Have you written more on this particular subject? And if you haven't, but were going to, what subjects would you look to?
Cousin Paul is the only piece I wrote on the subjects of Paul McCartney or Ireland. I do not foresee that I will be writing any farther on either of these subjects.

In recent years I enjoyed writing literary short stories and I have had modest successes in that genre. My topics have been developed mostly from subjects that pop into my head. I cannot generalize, but it seems many of the stories I published have a right-versus-wrong theme.

Would it be correct to assume you are a fan of the Beetles and, more particularly, Paul McCartney?
I believe Paul McCartney is a gifted artist who has delighted millions of people with his music. However, I have never been a fan of pop music of any type. I admire and respect Paul for his tremendous achievements, and I would be delighted to hang one of his signed photographs on my family room wall. So, in that regard you could say I am a fan of his. Truth be told, I am more into the works of Schubert, Chopin, Tchaikovsky and the like.

Novice Bank Robber
(A fictional short story)

Although it is early afternoon Mason Berger is still in his PJ's and watching TV. Children's cartoons, actually. A knock at the apartment door startles him. Walking to the door, he opens it a crack to see who might be there. It is Mildred Barnes, the landlady, displaying a frown.

"Oh, hello, Missus Barnes."

"Mason, you are behind on the rent again. I must tell you I am getting tired of chasing after you every month. I don't have that problem with anyone else in the building. Let me put it to you in a few words. If I don't get your rent money by Saturday, your belongings will be moved to the sidewalk in front of the building. Sunshine, rain, hoodlums or whatever. It doesn't matter to me. And the lock on your door will be changed. Good day!"

Mason does not say anything in response. He has nothing to say. He also has no rent money.

Mrs. Barnes does a quick about face. The sound of heavy footsteps on the wooden floor punctuates her determination. Mason slowly closes the apartment door and decides it is time for a beer or two, something to help stir up some fresh ideas.

After slipping into jeans, sandals and the least soiled of the T-shirts, Mason shuffles to the local watering hole. At the bar he takes a seat next to two men who appear to be newcomers.

Bartender Eric slowly walks over to Mason. Eric basically does not like Mason, his loud talk or his boisterous ways. Nevertheless, he is willing to accept Mason's money this day as he has many days in the past.

"The usual?"

"Yeah."

Eric draws a draft beer and places it in front of Mason. Foam runs down the side of the glass and slops onto the counter. Eric makes no effort to soak up the spilled foam.

"How's it going, Mason?"

"Not good. Not good at all."

Mason's comments come as no surprise to Eric. In fact, he cannot remember Mason ever saying things were going well. The two men next to Mason lift their glasses in Eric's direction, and Eric moves over to draw them each a fresh draft. It is obvious that Mason wants to talk. Taking his time, Eric washes a few glasses and then returns to Mason.

"Problems, Mason?"

"I lost my job a few weeks ago. The boss caught me taking a wrench. I've been looking for another job, but it's tough out there. Very few jobs anywhere."

Mason makes no mention of the various prospective employers who showed an initial interest. In every case the interest went away when the background report arrived. Mostly, the breaking and entering seemed to be the big hindrance.

Eric pretends to be concerned and compassionate.

"Too bad! Couldn't you have come up with a cock-and-bull story of some sort? You know. Like, couldn't you say you were only going to borrow the wrench to fix a drain at home? You were going to bring it back the next day. Maybe he would have gone for it."

"No, I don't think so. He caught me red-handed. He had it in for me anyhow. No, this is it. I have no idea what I'm going to do now. Maybe I'll come up with something."

Eventually Mason finishes his first beer. Since Mason always has more than one beer Eric refills his glass without asking.

Three water company workers enter and move to a table near the front door, marking their path with muddy footprints. Eric, pleased for the excuse to escape from Mason, walks over to take their orders while casting side glances at the mud on his floor.

"Digging up the street again, guys?"

The men look at one another but say nothing in response.

"Bring us each two Budweisers."

Obviously the water company workers do not trust draft beer.

Drinking alone at the bar, Mason contemplates his dilemma. He realizes that if he does not come up with some cash soon, he will be living on the streets. Eating at church kitchens–again. He is becoming dejected with his plight. Sipping his beer, Mason finds he can easily hear the conversation of the men next to him. The nearest man is talking about a local bank chain.

"I don't get it. Some higher-ups at Spanner's headquarters told the local managers that the guns must go. Up until last week they had an armed guard at the front door of every branch office. The bank never had a robbery at any of its branches. I think they became worried about liability and getting sued. Anyway, I'll bet they will have some unwelcomed visitors in the near future."

From their discussion it becomes apparent that the two men are off-duty policemen.

The man next to Mason drains his glass and throws some bills on the bar. He tells Eric, "Got to go."

Together the policemen exit the bar. The man who was next to Mason tells his friend,

"I'm on duty in half an hour. See you tomorrow."

The policeman's comments catch Mason's attention. Definitely food for thought! After some rumination on the subject Mason concludes that, really, his only remaining option is to rob a bank, one free of armed guards. He reasons his past experience with breaking and entering would be of some help. That was easy! Robbing a bank could not be all that much more difficult. It might even be easier.

After Mason downs another beer he decides it is time for action. It's a good day for a visit to a Spanner Bank. He decides he needs money more than the bank does. A Spanner Bank on the other side of town seems to be a good prospect. Over there the chances of his being recognized are less. He pays his tab and heads for the door, bumping into a chair near the door.

"See you, Eric."

"See you, Mason."

Mason returns to his apartment where he exchanges sandals for shoes. Something better for running. In the pile of dirty clothing he picks out a rumpled shirt and puts it over the T-shirt. Oh, yes. Shades might be a good idea. And a hoodie for good measure. He enters his 1988 Chevy and cranks the engine. At first the old car is reluctant to start. It has been parked on the street and unused for weeks. After a few coughs and spits the engine finally starts. Driving to the south side of town he maneuvers into a parking spot two blocks from a Spanner Bank branch office.

Entering the bank Mason looks around carefully. There is no guard of any type in sight. That's consoling. He sees there are five windows but only three are attended by tellers. One is a young, pretty brunette. That one, he figures, might be more easily intimidated than the others and more cooperative. Mason walks up to the young lady.

"May I help you, sir?"

Mason looks around the bank before responding.

"Yes, I would like to make a withdrawal."

With a shaking hand and a nervous smile he pushes a crumpled note and a cloth bag across the marble counter to her.

The young teller does as the note demands. To Mason she does not appear in the least flustered. Maybe she has done this before? She has only $600 to give the novice robber. Barely enough for one month's rent and a few burgers. Slowly she places money in the bag and, while displaying a broad smile, moves her left foot over to press the silent alarm button. Beads of sweat appear on Mason's forehead as the alcohol-induced bravery starts to wane. His heart is pounding. He begins to have doubts about this afternoon's outing.

With the bag in hand, Mason turns and walks out of the bank. His legs tell him to run, but he forces himself to walk. Running would certainly draw unwanted attention. On the sidewalk, he moves briskly toward the parked Chevy. Meanwhile police cruisers are speeding to the area. Entering his car, Mason inserts the key in the ignition. But the damned steering wheel is locked in position. This has happened on occasion in the past. Pulling, pushing and cursing the thing does nothing. It will not budge. He begins to believe that perhaps it would be better to merely walk away and return for the car another day? One last try! A hard pull to the left, and the wheel finally comes free. He cranks the engine. It will not start. Another try and another. It finally catches.

Before pulling out of the parking spot, Mason turns his head to be certain the way is clear. This would not be a good time to have an accident. A black car is approaching and Mason waits. It is an unmarked police car, and the policeman is driving slowly as he notices the wheels on a vehicle turned to exit a parking spot. He pulls up beside Mason's Chevy. The policeman in the vehicle looks over at Mason and their eyes meet. Mason whispers, "Oh shit."

It is the policeman who was next to Mason at the bar a short time earlier. The policeman immediately recognizes Mason. At the same time he realizes that the man in the old Chevy had not only heard his tale about the guns, but also saw him drinking beer before going on duty. He tells himself that if that man was brought in and questioned there could be some resulting and adverse entries made to the file. Those entries could do serious and lasting damage to a policeman's career. And, too, there are mortgage payments to be considered.

The policeman decides he should look for the bank robber elsewhere. Perhaps in the next block? Slowly returning his gaze to the street ahead, he moves his vehicle forward. Mason takes a deep breath and exhales slowly. After the black car disappears around the corner, he, too, drives away.

On the return trip to his apartment, Mason tells himself, "That does it! No more bank robberies."

Pretend Love
(A fictional short story)

Wally spotted Sean McDougal behind the counter as he walked into the gun shop.

"Hey, Sean."

"Yo, Wally."

Wally came by McDougal's Firearms frequently, although at unpredictable times. On occasion he dusted the guns, swept the floor or cleaned the windows. Although Sean liked having Wally around, the two were very much opposites. Maybe that was why they were the best of friends. In a way, they were a modern-day Bud Abbot-Lou Costello.

Sean, the straight guy, was the thinker and businessman. He went to the gym every other day and ate mostly organic food. While in the Army, he did all right as a boxer. Wally, on the other hand, didn't care about money, fame or success. He did things when the mood moved him, not when others thought he should. He smoked, preferred junk food, and didn't care for exercise of any type.

Sean finished writing in a ledger and looked up.

"Strange thing happened today. Two guys were waiting in the parking lot when I came to open up. Said they were CIA."

"Wow. You didn't sell any illegal guns or anything, did you?"

"Of course not! I'm not that stupid. They said they wanted to talk with me about something. Asked me to visit their office in Frederick. They gave me a business card."

"You goin' to see them?"

"Yeah, out of curiosity, if nothing else. Maybe all they want is to buy a lot of guns. If so, I'll help them there." With a smile, Sean rubbed his thumb and index finger together.

***

As arranged, Sean drove to Frederick. In the lobby of the high-rise, He looked for a listing of CIA but didn't see one. The business card said: Suite 803. On the eighth floor, he opened the Office 803 door. The man who had identified himself as Bryan Gibson greeted Sean. Standing at his full six feet-one, he told Sean that his services were needed to: "take out a known terrorist before the man could kill innocent Americans.

"All you need to do is enter the woods on the opening day of the deer season in Pennsylvania. Here's a detailed map. You'll find the target, Kalid Uznitsky, in a treestand. There will be an unfortunate hunting accident. Afterwards, you casually walk out of the woods. The following day, you will be paid $50,000, courtesy of the US Government."

Sean blinked, said nothing, took the map and left.

Sean returned to the gun shop mid-afternoon. Wally was behind the counter in one of his staring moods. It happened often. Wally was seemingly concentrating on the mounted eight point buck on the front wall, but mentally off in space somewhere and far removed from the present. Maybe it wasn't the dusty buck's head on the wall, but memories about a time when enemy bullets were flying around and death was a genuine possibility. Sean never commented and Wally never offered an explanation.

"Sell any guns, Wally?"

"What? Oh, yes, one."

Wally stammered, embarrassed. "An old German Mauser. A farmer wanted a cheap rifle to shoot deer eating his corn. Hey, how did it go with the CIA?"

"They said they want me to drill some guy in the back, all for the good of America. They promised there would be $50,000 in it for me. "Wow! You goin' to do it?"

"Monday I'll be 'hunting in the woods' near this guy. You're going to help me. This is going to be an adventure that you and I will never forget. I promise."

***

Monday was the opening of deer season in Pennsylvania's woods and, as usual, there were hundreds of hunters in the woods. Almost to a man, they were decked out in the standard orange parkas and hats. Some were hunting a trophy buck and bragging rights. Others were merely after cheap meat for the table. The intended victim, who had been identified as Kalid Uznitsky, had been in his treestand since well before daylight, hoping for his first-day buck.

Shortly after dawn, Sean pulled his car beyond the one that he was told would be Kalid's. He loaded his .306 caliber rifle, entered the woods and climbed carefully to the ridge crest above Uznitsky's location. At mid-morning, Wally drove up the same road and parked. He was wearing a green jacket and matching trousers that resembled the uniforms worn by the Pennsylvania Game Wardens. A patch on his left shoulder made the outfit look almost official. He walked in, straight for Uznitsky's treestand. Standing below the intended victim, he called out, "You up there. Unload your rifle and come down."

The man up in the treestand was dumbfounded. He wanted no problems with lawmen. He answered, "Yes, sir."

As instructed, he unloaded his rifle and climbed down the ladder. Once on ground level, he looked incredulously at the man he took to be a waiting game warden.

Wally asked in his "official" voice: "Could I see your hunting license and driver's license?"

Both licenses showed the name "Boris Brednisky." Wally made notes and returned the documents. "Sorry for the interruption. Just doing my job. Hope you get a big buck today."

In an accent that sounded Russian, he replied, "Thank you veyy much."

Boris Brednisky, relieved, returned to his perch in the treestand. Wally continued into the woods as he pretended to look for more hunters. Once out of sight, Wally circled back to his car, and called Sean on his cell phone.

"Yo. What's up?"

"The driver's license and the hunting license both say his name is Boris Brednisky. I got his address. He <u>does</u> have a Russian accent."

"You did well, Wally. See you in the shop, say, around eleven tonight? Park around back. I'm staying out here to make it look real. I don't know who is watching."

"Sure. See you later."

***

That night, Wally came in the back door of the gun shop. Sean was waiting in the little office.

"You should consider an acting career. Anyway, did the guy seem anyway suspicious?"

"Nah. To me, he seemed like another immigrant, just happy to be in the good old US of A. He sure didn't have the look of a terrorist to me."

"That name is different than the one the CIA guys gave me. I don't know what's going on but you and I are going to figure this thing out one way or the other."

"What do you mean one way or the other? I told you I don't want any trouble messing up my monthly disability checks."

"Wally, you're fine. Trust me. You've nothing to worry about."

Sean paused. "Listen. I have a plan of sorts here. Before you came in, I called the CIA guy and told him I couldn't get a clean shot today, but I'll give it another try Wednesday. He didn't like what I had to say, but I told him that's the way it's going to be. We need a day to get organized. I did something else. I called a private detective I know. He's going to put a tap on the telephone at Boris' home. Maybe we can learn something."

***

Sean was in his gun shop the second day of deer season. The sign in the window said "Open." But it was a slow day, worse than slow. Not a single potential customer walked through the front door. Late afternoon, he received a call from the private investigator who had tapped Boris Brednisky's phone.

"Got some intel for you. This Boris Brednisky. His wife goes by the name of Tanya but that's not her real name. More on that later. It seems the hubby is out hunting today and she placed a call to some guy and asked, "How did it go?"

"The guy said that it didn't go down yet, but he expects it will Wednesday. She sounded pissed and was shouting sailor words into the phone. She and Boris are married, which suggests something. My bill's now $2,000. Need any more?"

"Yeah. Leave the tap on for at least one more day."

"Can do."

Sean hung up and yelled, "Wally, we have things to do."

***

On Wednesday Sean went to the ridge above Boris' treestand again exactly as he told the CIA types that he would. Boris was standing in the snow below the treestand. At 10 a.m., a shot ran out from Sean's rifle. Boris fell to the ground, his rifle beside him. In time, someone called an ambulance and the body, covered with a sheet, was carried out of the woods. The ambulance disappeared up the road with its cargo.

Sean called the CIA number at noon. A woman answered.

"CIA. May I help you?"

"Hi. This is Sean McDougal. Is Bryan there?"

"No, sir. Agent Gibson is out of the office on business, but he said I should give you a message. He said one of our men reported you did good work. If you would come to the office at 2 p.m. today, he will have a package for you."

"Oh, okay. I'll be there at two."

Sean replaced the handset in the receiver and it rang immediately. It was the private detective.

"Sean, got something of interest. Somebody called Boris' home and the lady answered. The guy said it was finished and that they should meet today. She suggested the McDonald's in Frederick at two this afternoon."

"That's all good stuff."

***

At 1 p.m., Sean and Wally parked in a lot near the McDonald's. About 1:45 p.m. a woman carrying a maroon briefcase and wearing dark glasses walked inside. At 2:00 p.m., sharp, the imitation CIA men pulled into the lot. One of the men, later identified as Bruno Spadafore, waited in the car. The man known as Bryan Gibson opened the car door and walked in.

Sean touched Wally's arm. "Let's go."

The man wore a dark jacket that probably allowed him to conceal something like a .38 revolver. He opened the front door cautiously, spotted the woman with the briefcase and walked towards her booth. Sean and Wally were close behind him. When Sean caught up with the man, he tapped him on the shoulder.

"Hello, Bryan."

The man turned, obviously surprised.

"Sean! Strange seeing you here. What a coincidence."

The woman saw the commotion near the front door and

recognized the man she knew as Bryan Gibson. Sensing trouble, she grabbed the briefcase and, eyeing the door, stood. Sean moved to block her path."

"Mrs. Brednisky, what say you have a seat so we can have a little chat?"

The woman was frozen in place for a long moment. Her eyes blinked a few times, then her shoulders sagged. "Sure. Let's talk."

Sean took out his cell phone and dialed.

"Come on in now. We're to the right as you enter."

Boris Brednisky, who had been waiting behind the building, entered the front door. The woman gasped. Boris walked over to the table.

"Hello Tanya. I still alive. You surprise see me?"

Tanya sat motionless, then began sobbing.

The sound of screeching tires in the parking lot caught the attention of everyone but Sean. The second so-called agent, actually Bruno Spadafore, was making his escape, leaving his cohort behind.

Bryan, speaking to no one in particular, declared, "That son of a ....."

Bryan moved a step closer to Sean. Boris began to speak to Tanya again.

"Tanya, I..."

Bryan used the distraction to try a gut punch on Sean, who was more than ready. The body armor under his jacket absorbed the impact. Sean hardly flinched. He waited a half-second for effect, then the left jab target was Bryan's nose. Bryan reeled, startled. A quick right jab slammed into the same nose, moving it sideways. He fell to the floor, dazed. With Wally's help Sean secured Bryan's hands behind him.

Tanya saw her chance, grabbed the briefcase and dashed for the door. As she went by, Wally extended his foot. Tanya went sprawling one way, while the briefcase went in another direction.

As she scrambled to her feet, Tanya had to make a quick decision. Go for the briefcase and sure capture–or go for the door and possible escape. She decided on the door.

Sean placed another call. Shortly, a uniformed policeman came in and took Bryan by the arm. This was obviously not the cop's first meeting with the man.

"In trouble again, hm? Let's go, Mario."

Boris retrieved the maroon briefcase from beneath the table and handed it to Sean. Russian style, he threw his arms around Sean and held him tightly in a bear hug.

"Here. You save my life. Whatever here you take."

At the booking, the so-called CIA agent, who previously went by the name of Bryan Gibson, gave his name as Mario Piconne from Philadelphia. On the new mug shot, his nose had a very different appearance from the one on file. Mario and enthusiastically identified has accomplice as Bruno Spadafore. He was released after a few days, as there was no usable evidence.

After the McDonald's event, Sean and Wally returned to the gun shop with the briefcase, which went on the counter, like a trophy.

"We need a beer, Wally. What do you think?"

"Sure. I think we earned one. Hey, maybe two."

Sean opened two Yuengling long necks and placed one in front of Wally.

They clinked bottles. Grinning, Sean leaned back in his chair: "Well, Wally, what do you think is in here?"

"How the hell should I know? Obviously, it was pay for a contract to take out Boris so that Tanya could, what, collect insurance money or maybe his whole estate? One or the other. Rather than get involved, Marco and Bruno were going to use you to do the dirty work."

"That was my thinking, too. Well, now…let's see."

Sean clicked the briefcase locks. The only items were two paper rolls, each marked with the number"100" and some Russian words. Each roll held 100 gold coins

Sean hefted one roll.

"I'll bet each of these is worth over $100,000."

They looked at one another without speaking a word.

Thinking out loud, Sean added: "I'll guess that Boris kept these in a safe deposit box somewhere and, somehow, Tanya got access to them."

Wally nodded. "Too bad. It seems he really loved her but she was only pretending at love."

Sean took the roll in hand and reached forward.

"What say you take one and I take one?"

"Oh, I don't know, Sean. You were the mastermind. Besides, I don't know what this would do to my disability checks."

"You're _going_ to take these. When you want cash, bring a few coins in here. I'll turn them into cash for you. I have ways. No one else will ever know."

"If you insist."

Wally took hold of the heavy roll of coins. As he admired it, the glint of a light reflection from the end coin seemed to endorse the value of his new possession.

"Gee, Sean, thanks. That's the greatest gift anyone ever gave me."

Sean gave a check to each of the two men who drove the ambulance and carried Boris out of the woods on a stretcher.

Sean placed the coins in a safe deposit box for possible future use. Wally did the same with his coins.

Tanya returned to Chicago and her job at the massage parlor. Boris told the policeman, "Tanya not bad girl. She jus' not know better. Not raised right. I vill miss her ver' much. I not press charge. No, maybe she come back one day."

A friend of Bruno Spadafore spotted him walking in South Philadelphia, a cane in one hand and a bandage over his nose.

"Hey, Bruno, wats a matter wit ya? Ya don't look sa good."

"Nut'n, I fell on da God damned house steps. At's all."

We, the ROTC Cadets
(A creative nonfiction short story)

Lieutenant Lowe accepted the report of "all present and accounted for." He returned the first sergeant's salute and his eyes drifted over the company of cadets. It seemed he felt no immediate obligation to say anything. The pause was for effect. Michael Hunter, standing next to me, whispered, "I wonder what torture Beauregard has in mind for us today."

Michael and I had become good friends while working our way through college and the four-year Reserve Officer Training Corp program. We had a lot in common, but mostly beer and coeds. The five-week long summer camp in which we found ourselves was an obligatory part of the ROTC program. More than anything, the summer camp was a test of a man's will, his physical endurance, and his suitability to be a leader.

Michael and I decided "Beauregard" was a suitable name for Lieutenant Lowe because he came from down south. He was also a "90-Day Wonder," which was cause for wariness. The wonders were once enlisted men who had applied for and made it through the 90-day Officer Candidate School. We tended to look down on the wonders in part because they were not college graduates. We had military courses during a four-year period, drills, and the mandatory five weeks of summer camp. Only if we completed the program successfully and received a bonafide college diploma would we be eligible for a commission. And then there would be another 14 weeks of training. The wonders resented ROTC cadets as smart-ass college boys, while we considered them to be only moderately trained officers.

Beauregard could have told us to be "at ease"– but he didn't. He allowed us to remain standing rigid with our hands at our sides, staring straight ahead into the distance. After a pause, he told the first sergeant he would inspect the second platoon. Those men were from Indiana, New Hampshire and Massachusetts, all Yankees to his way of thinking. With both the first sergeant and the second platoon sergeant in tow, he slowly weaved through the ranks. He sought out those cadets who seemed to lack the physical and mental requirements of being a US Army officer. It was a task he relished.

"A gig for Hendrickson," Beauregard said. "His belt buckle needs a shine." The first sergeant, himself a cadet filling that role for the day, recorded the gigs in a notebook. "Another for Gibson. His hat is tilted to the side of this head. This is the United States Army and not a Vaudeville show." Too many gigs and a cadet would no longer be a cadet. He'd go home. No one wanted the shame. While the lieutenant was taking his time, we were becoming tired from standing stiffly at attention in the stifling heat.

Beauregard returned to a position in front of the company. "Have the men collect their packs, half a tent, a rifle and return here at ten hundred hour," he told the first sergeant. "Then march them to Camp A." Beauregard sauntered off and disappeared behind the mess hall.

We were each issued a rifle and a bayonet but no bullets. A meticulous army supply sergeant, a genuine US Army sergeant, recorded our name and the serial number of the rifle handed to each cadet. Michael, who was in line in front of me, asked the supply sergeant, "What in the hell am I supposed to do with a rifle with no bullets?"

"Mister, I don't give a shit what you do with the rifle," the sergeant told him. "I was told to give you guys a rifle and that is what I am doing. I'll be here tomorrow and I'll expect you to return that rifle in good condition."

Waiting near the assembly area, we sat on our packs in the shade of the nearest barracks. At the designated time, we headed out toward a new adventure in a column of two led by our platoon sergeant, who had a quick step. The road had been driven over by tanks, which had pulverized the dirt into a powder five inches deep. The two men at the head of the column were alright but behind them the dirt rose in large yellow billows. We breathed and ate dirt by the handful. The sun beat down and our sweat mixed with the dust. The resulting mud clung to skin, nostrils and clothing.

After two hours of non-stop marching, we arrived at a large grass field surrounded by old oak trees. A sign in the middle of the field declared the area to be "Camp A." We resembled a platoon of coal miners, except the coloration was brown instead of black. Sitting in a Jeep parked in the shade, Beauregard watched the proceedings. He told our platoon sergeant to have his men pitch their tents at the south end of the field. We would be bivouacking there overnight. We all desperately wanted to wash away the mud but nobody cared to be the first to suggest water. Nobody wanted to draw attention to their person. I suspected Beauregard was enjoying himself.

In the afternoon, real Army sergeants with genuine stripes and rockers on their sleeves held classes on the topic of river crossings. We are the Corp of Engineers and getting soldiers over rivers is our responsibility, they told us. The mess truck did not appear for lunch. A sergeant, who implied that he spoke from battlefield experience, explained that in combat soldiers sometimes found it necessary to forfeit meals. So, he added, it would be good practice for officers-to-be. Late in the evening a mess truck appeared, and we ate like starved wolves.

After supper, the first sergeant told us that at midnight we were to form up in squads. Another hike! At Camp B, along the western bank of the Potomac River, we would find boats, with which we would launch an attack against a well prepared enemy on the opposite bank. Michael and I returned to our tent and immediately lay down to catch some rest. We were tired from the march and the sweltering heat. The mosquitoes and the black flies were competing for our blood.

At midnight, a three-stripe Army sergeant gave us a compass azimuth for Camp B, a mile away through the woods, and told us to head out. Our squad consisted of eight men. Two came from New York City and four were from Maine. Michael and I were Pennsylvanians. Somehow, one of the guys from New York got the compass and a small flashlight. The sergeant designated him as our leader and the cadet declared he "could handle this."

After an hour we were still wandering around in the woods, but we eventually we found our way to Camp B, where the rest of the company was already stretched out on the grass amongst the tics and ants. We found space and settled in.

Eventually, the first sergeant told us to move out to the boats and start across the river, one squad per boat. He added that the crossing was to be silent and there was to be no loud talking. Getting eight men into a boat became a problem. The flat-bottomed boats could swamp easily if too much weight was put on one side. Once away from the bank the constant sound of rifles smacking boat sides filled the air. We headed for the "enemy" on the east side of the river. A little beyond the half-way point there was a loud ruckus and shouting. One of the boats overturned, dumping a squad into the water. We all kept moving to our "objective." We figured they could either cling to the boat or swim.

When we neared the opposite bank, machine-gun fire erupted in our direction. The muzzle flashes indicated three machine-gun nests, all firing blanks. We knew that the Army would not wish to shoot to kill us, considering the amount of time and money they had already invested in each of us. No one feared for his life. The boat to our right arrived at the river bank a little ahead of us. Then our boat hit land. A man from the first boat ran up to the machine gunner and pulled him from behind the gun. He shouted, "You son of a bitch! You hit me in the face with those God-damned blanks." The cadet swung at the guy, an enlisted man, but missed. The two men became the only true combatants of the evening.

Michael, who was the first out of our boat, took a few steps and shouted, "There's a big fucking snake here." He ran up the bank and disappeared out of sight. Michael hated snakes. I was next to last out. A few feet from the boat, some kind of small animal ran in front of me and stopped, challenging me to come closer. Whatever it was, I walked around it. My personal objective was to get through the night without serious encounters, injuries or gigs.

Eventually, someone sounded a whistle, marking the end of our attack, and we all gathered around a barrel-chested Army sergeant. Headlights from Beauregard's Jeep illuminated a small area in the middle of a field. The sergeant told us to get back in the boats and return to the other side of the river. "Reveille will be at six hundred hour," he said. Nothing about "I know you are all tired, so get your sleep." No, a real sergeant would not talk like that.

I jumped into the first boat that had an empty seat and we pushed off for the western bank and Camp B. None of the men were from my squad. Once in the tent, I lay down in my uniform, too tired to bother removing my soaked boots and socks. Because I did not wish to pay for a lost rifle, I kept my rifle next to me in the tent. Michael climbed in the tent while I was sleeping.

Next morning when count was taken, two men were missing from the second platoon. Later, we learned they were in the boat that capsized during the assault. They had lost the oars to the boat and drifted with the boat downstream. When they returned to camp two days later, they were told to pack their bags and go home. Another cadet lost his rifle in the river and had to pay for it. Beauregard gave the cadet four gigs for that. The Army very much did not like to see a soldier separated from his rifle.

After lunch, Beauregard inspected the company, starting with our platoon. As he weaved between the rows, now and then he would scan a cadet from cap to shoe. He stopped in front of me, paused, and asked, "Where you from, mista?" I knew he didn't care about the city. He was interested in the state. "Pennsylvania, sir." In response he told me, "Let me see your bayonet." I retrieved the bayonet from the sheaf at my left side and held it in front of me, resting on both hands. I knew the bayonet was in good condition, because I had given it a good cleaning that morning. Beauregard took the bayonet and turned it over. "This chir thing is one of the worst I ever seen. One gig," he told the first sergeant. Beauregard was baiting me, but I said nothing. He handed the weapon back to me. I replaced it in my sheaf and stood at attention, waiting. He paused, then slowly stepped down the line.

Beauregard grew tired of playing with us and we marched back to the barracks. Most of us had had only an hour or two of sleep. Some of us still had wet boots and socks. We all had dozens of welts from the insects. The march back was tiring, but we all made it.

It took most of the morning for the supply sergeant to accept the rifles. He was fussy and made some cadets clean and oil their guns two or three times. The coating of oil had to be just right: not too thick and not too thin. And definitely no sign of oil on the rifle's stock.

Two days after the river crossing, Michael told me he was itchy all over, particularly on his private parts. Large red blotches covered his hands and face. He said he was going to see one of the horse doctors. I couldn't determine which he disliked more: snakes or army doctors. After a couple of days, when Michael hadn't returned, I went to the dispensary to inquire. A nurse led me to a room where Michael was sitting in a bathtub full of some kind of solution up to his neck. He wore only a pair of briefs. "What the hell?" I said.

"I got poison ivy all over my body. It itches like a son of a bitch," he said. "They make me stay in this bath all day long. At night I sleep in a bed, but that's almost worse because the itching gets really bad."

"Look at it on the bright side," I said. "Now you are excused from the long hikes in choking dust."

He laughed and told me, "I'll take the dirt."

Michael said Beauregard had visited him at the dispensary to let him know he didn't do anything out of line. Without becoming too sentimental, he told Michael he "will be alright" and that he was "a good soldier." Michael stayed in the hospital until the summer camp came to an end four weeks later. Beauregard gave him a "pass." During those weeks, and more of Beauregard's tests, I began to enjoy summer camp, the challenges and the camaraderie. I convinced myself I could handle anything Beauregard might have for me. In fact, I suspected I could enjoy a stint as an army officer.

On the last day in camp everyone reported one at a time to Beauregard in his office. We heard that Beauregard decided five cadets in our company were unsuitable officer material, and he dropped them from the program. Sometimes it was due to too many gigs but mostly for no stated reason. The officer's decision was final. There was no board of appeal, no means to submit a complaint. It's how the army functions.

When my turn came, I didn't know what to expect. I entered and saluted. He told me "at ease." It was the first time I had heard him utter those words. In due time, he told me that I passed and congratulated me. "Thank you, sir." I said, and he responded with a "dismissed." If I completed one more year of the ROTC program and received a diploma, I would be awarded a commission as a second lieutenant.

On the last day at camp, Michael and I were given bus money for a return trip to Pittsburgh. But there was an ample supply of drivers willing to give a ride to young men in uniform. We kept the money and thumbed our way home.

Gobblers and Grapes
(A creative nonfiction short story)

I locked the doors of my SUV, slid some shells into the 12-gauge shotgun and started hiking out a trail between two long mountain ridges. The morning promised to be one of the most gorgeous of the year. Most of the leaves had fallen, the sun was shinning and a slight chill hung in the air. I knew I would enjoy the day whether I found any turkeys or not.

In past years I had encountered turkeys in the valley ahead, and I thought there would be some there this day. But after three hours of walking, I hadn't found any scratchings or other turkey sign. I had intended to continue out the valley for another hour and then return to my vehicle along the top of the ridge to the south, but the complete lack of sign led me to reconsider my plans.

As I was trying to decide on a course of action, I remembered that the previous week I had seen what might have been turkey scratchings on the ridge to the south. The marks could have been made by deer pawing for acorns, but as I thought about it I recalled the presence of wild grapes in the area. I had noticed some of the dried grape bunches had fallen to the forest floor. Turkeys feed mostly on acorns, but wild grapes are also high on their list of favorite foods. With nothing to lose, I decided to head there immediately and have a look around.

It took me half an hour to climb to the summit of the ridge, and on the way I called occasionally, hoping to walk within earshot of a flock. I use only a kee-kee because it seems to put the birds at ease. My intention is to simulate a lost bird looking for a flock. I often peek over the edges of the hills or from behind laurels and spot them. I've found old birds this way as well as young ones.

But this day the woods remained silent. Upon reaching the crest of the ridge, I slowly zigzagged across the summit–calling, walking to one edge and looking. Then I would repeat the process on the other side of the ridge top.

Just 200 yards from my destination, a knoll blocked my view of the area. I repeated the lost call before climbing the rise, and as I reached the crest, a magnificent gobbler flushed only 40 yards away. I was awed by its huge black body and long beard, and it was a sight I'll never forget.

Immediately after the gobbler flushed, about eight young birds flew out about 30 yards from where the gobbler had been. I could distinguish the young birds from the mature birds by their more rapid wing beats. The gobble had flow through the timber to my left, whereas the young birds flew down the hill to my right. The scene I witnessed baffled me because mature gobblers don't normally travel with young birds, and I saw no sign of a mother hen. Obviously the birds were feeding on the wild grapes in the area.

I decided to set up against a large oak near were the gobbler had flushed. I put on my face mask. Together with my other camo clothing, the turkeys should have difficulty spotting me. I noticed it was 11:15. All the rules say the mature gobblers hang out with only other mature gobblers so I thought the scenario I had come across was a little unusual. Perhaps, I thought, the large gobbler I had seen had become separated from his bachelor buddies and decided to temporarily associated with the flock of young birds.

I figured I'd never see the flock of young birds again. They flew away down a steep hill and in a tight group. It seemed unlikely I would have any success in calling them up the hill again. My best bet lay with the gobbler.

Mature Gobblers are known to be very cautious and slow to regroup. Sometimes they do not get together for a day or two. And to make things more difficult, this one was not part of a bachelor group. Still, it was the only game in town. I considered making an adult gobbler call, but I thought that might make him suspicious. He had just been with young birds, so it seemed to me that a young bird call should not spook him. A half hour after I had flushed the gobbler, I started to call. I gave one kee-kee call and listened. No response.

I leaned back against the trunk of the oak and glazed at the beautiful blue sky. I watched squirrels and songbirds for a while. With five hours until sundown I debated whether to stay or move. While I was weighing my options, I heard two course yelps over my left shoulder. It was the gobbler.

I waited about 20 seconds and answered with two reassuring clucks. Shortly I heard the leaves rustling and then the gobbler's head and neck appeared 30 yards away.

The gobbler walked behind a laurel busk as he looked left and right. When he walked out the other side I was ready. One shot and he was down. Walking over to claim my prize, I immediately realized he was by far the largest gobbler I had ever bagged.

When I turned him over, I was surprised by the length of his beard. It measured 11-1/2 inches. Friends of mine who say I never show emotion should have seen my little victory dance.

After tagging the bird, I took a section of cord from my shoulder bag and tied it between the bird's feet to serve as a handle. It was more than a mile back to my vehicle and I wanted to bring the gobbler out of the woods in good condition. I already knew the bird's beard and fanned tail feathers would be displayed in a place of honor in my family room. When I opened the gobbler's gizzard later I found a mixture of acorns and, as I expected, wild grapes. There were not many grape vines on that ridge, but the turkeys had found them. And so did I.

The Snow Queen Contest
(A creative nonfiction short story)

The ski club's first meeting of the year is always exciting, festive. Friends and acquaintances from past trips would be there. There would be the retelling of encountered experiences from the previous ski season, as well as those from the summer months. There was always anticipation of the announcements of upcoming trips. A speaker would address a subject of common interest. Occasionally, a local ski shop would provide a fashion show to display their goods. There is always the man-woman thing, guys on the chase and women looking sideways now and then.

The club had over one thousand members although only a fraction of the members attended meetings. The club held the meetings in a rear room of a popular restaurant. A bar was located just outside the room, and it was well patronized by the club's members before, during and after the meetings. The building's owner never charged the club for use of the room. He made enough from the bar sales. Skiers tend to be a robust, don't-give-a-damn, thirsty lot. It was almost as though you can't fit in unless you are an imbiber.

Once the president announced the meeting was about to start, some members finished their drinks. Others scurried out for a fresh one to have while they paid attention to the club's proceedings. After most were seated and the chatter decreased somewhat, the president started the meeting. Half way through the "new business," the club president, Ryan, made an announcement that startled me. He told the group I would be chairman of the annual Snow Queen Contest. Those present responded with a hearty round of applause. I smiled and waved a hand in the air to let everyone know I was present. I couldn't merely sit there, stone-faced. In truth, I didn't know what to make of the news. I thought it strange that Ryan hadn't asked me in advance if I wanted the assignment. As I shall explain, I was pitifully naïve.

It was true. I had become one of the Club's more active members and an enthusiastic supporter of its events. I was the club's treasurer the previous year, and I helped with many of the club's activities. Being a bachelor I had the time. I started to suspect the assignment as chairmanship of the Snow Queen Contest was intended as a reward for my service to the club.

The evening Ryan appointed me chairman of the Snow Queen Contest, as was my custom, I stayed around after the formal meeting for a few beers and chatter. With beer glass in hand, I worked my way over to where Ryan was mingling with friends. I thought I should thank him for what appeared to be a favor. It seemed to be the right thing to do. When I caught his eye, I told him, "Say, Ryan, I want to thank you."

Ryan responded with a broad smile that clearly showed most of the teeth in his mouth.

"Joe, you earned it."

Ryan, too, seemed especially happy for me. His comment confirmed what I suspected: The Club intended the chairmanship as a bonus. It was a favor, not a chore. It gradually occurred to me that, yes, I might enjoy this adventure.

***

I resolved I would take my role as Snow Queen chairman seriously. I would be conscientious and do whatever was necessary to make the contest a success. My first efforts would be to promote the event. Because I would need entrants, I called the club's secretary and asked her to place a notice in the monthly newsletter. I told her to say the Snow Queen contest will be in March. Mention that no experience is required, and there will be a prize for the winner. To register, the girls should call me. I gave the secretary my phone number so that it may be included in the advertisement.

The ad in the newsletter brought calls from a few of the club's young women. Although several prospective entrants expressed curiosity, none committed to entering the contest. A typical call was the one I received from Ann, a friend of many years.

"Hi, Joe. How are you? I didn't have a chance to speak with you at the last meeting."

"Fine, Ann. Thanks. How about yourself? Maybe we will be on more trips together this year."

"Oh, I hope so. I can't wait for snow. I'm really looking forward to going on a trip or two. I couldn't wait for the summer to be over."

Of course, I knew the reason for Ann's call. She continued. "By the way, I see you are running the Snow Queen Contest this year."

Ann sounded different from the Ann I knew in the past. She had become upbeat, cheerful, so happy to talk with me. I tried to bring the level of conversation to a normal tone–to the way people usually talk to one another.

"Yes. You know that if there were no volunteers to run the club's activities, there would be no club. I'm only trying to do my part."

"Well, I think the club picked the right man for the job. I'm sure you will do a good job and be impartial."

I started to think Ann might be of the opinion that there is nothing wrong with a little partiality between friends. I told her, "To tell the truth, Ann, I am not going to be the judge. No, that would be too hazardous. I plan to have some older men be the judges. I'm merely the organizer. That way I get to live to ski down more hillsides."

"You're a smart guy. I was thinking of entering the contest. I haven't decided yet. I wanted to ask you a question or two. If I enter, what do you think I should wear? Something with a skiing motif? After-ski togs or something like that?"

I didn't care to sound too earnest or serious about my task as chairman. The event was intended to be a lighthearted affair, entertainment for all.

"Wear anything you wish. Short-shorts might be a good idea. If you want to stand out you might try a G-string below and pasties up above. Just kidding. Be yourself and turn on the charm. I guess the judges would like to see a genuine smile and, I'm sure, skin."

"You men are all alike. I may or may not enter the contest. I'm not sure. See you later."

***

Starting with the November meeting, I was the recipient of comments from some of my friends—mostly jealous male friends. Michael was one of those friends. In many ways, Michael and I were two men of the same inclinations. Together, we had schussed down distant snow-covered slopes, drank beer and chased snow bunnies. Michael sought me out at the meeting, and, maneuvering me aside, asked, "How's the contest going?" He showed half a smile and seemed strangely curious.

I didn't know where he was going with this. I told him, "Ok, I guess. A few girls called me with questions. Some wanted to know what to wear, but that was about it. No girl has yet told me she plans to be in the contest."

"Really? You didn't tell them you would like to meet with them before the evening of the event? You know, to interview them and maybe have a drink somewhere? To give them some hints on what to wear. Hints as to what it might take to win?"

"No, I told them the prize is a sweater. I suggested that the judges would probably like to see legs."

Michael shifted to a frown and a whisper while squeezing my arm, I guessed, for emphasis. He looked around before speaking, much as though the two of us were about to cook up treachery.

"Joe, I'm disappointed in you. You should get up close to the girls. This is a rare opportunity. Some girls will do anything to win at a contest like this. You know what I mean. I'm talking anything!"

"No, I didn't look at it that way. Besides, I have a steady."

Michael was disappointed in me.

***

Several weeks before the contest, I contacted three political acquaintances and asked each if he would like being a judge of the contest. I did not need to beg.

One week before the March meeting, there were no applicants. I began to worry. Then the telephone started to ring. The girls had a variety of questions. How many have signed up so far? Will the names of the "losers" be in the newsletter? I told all of them the same: Show up the evening of the March meeting wearing whatever is your preference. Short-shorts might be a good idea. A local ski shop will be giving a good quality ski sweater to the Queen.

The night of the contest, one of the judges called and said he was unable to make it. Said he had forgotten about another commitment. I suspected he was afraid of losing the votes of disgruntled contestants. I decided to proceed with the two judges who had already committed. It was a mistake. The evening of the Snow Queen Contest, five girls, including my good friend Ann, approached me and said they would like to participate. Although it was a cold evening, all of the girls were wearing high cut shorts. Some of the shorts were made of material the thickness of crepe paper. The women's dress confirmed my long-held belief that skiers of both sexes were a reckless type.

I waited until the Club's president announced that the meeting was about to begin and "please take your seats." I led the parade of contestants and judges down the side of the main hall and to a private room in the basement. What a parade! The clicking of high heels on the wooden floor punctuated the show. A few men applauded. In the basement, I repeated the prize and the procedure for the contest. The rules, I explained, were simple. The judges will select the winner. I was greeted with smiles a plenty. The girls loved me.

One of the contestants, Ashley, said she had a question.

"What are we being judged on?"

I had to think quickly. Visions of pits with sharpened stakes pointing upward flashed through my mind.

I responded, "It's up to the judges. I would say that the winner would be a girl who is generally attractive and interesting. Skiing ability does not matter." Saying more, I concluded, would only risk unneeded danger.

Ashley had a response to which I had no possible comeback.

"Well, we all have THAT."

I realized I was in a predicament. What kind of an answer was she expecting? *Well, Ashley, in my opinion a well-developed set of tits might help. Or, a nicely shaped ass wouldn't hurt the cause. What about movie star looks?* Comments, almost any spoken words, could bring me trouble that might endure long into the future. I was about to speak when another of the contestants, Carol, addressed the subject.

"Ashley, we all have THAT but some of us have more of THAT than others."

I suspected Carol spoke up as a favor to me. Maybe she was hoping for points. Or, perhaps she was jumping at an opportunity to trash the competition. There was no way of telling.

Ashley's mouth dropped and it seemed she was about to comment further, possibly with spicy vulgarities. It occurred to me that Ashley might be of a type that would enjoy using sailor words on occasion. Instead, she held back and a broad smile replaced the frown. It was time for me to turn the discussion in another direction and without delay.

I told the group, "Girls, this is what we will do. The judges will interview one girl at a time while the others can join the regular meeting or have a drink at the bar. Drinks are on the club. When the judges have finished interviewing one girl, I will bring in the next one and so forth. The winner will be announced near the end of the regular meeting."

As I turned to go upstairs, I heard the judges trying to decide which contestant to interview first. The monthly meetings usually lasted about an hour and a half. There was much to be treated at the March meeting: the financial report, old business, new business, stories from recent trips, and a speaker who was demonstrating how skiers can wax their skis at home. After an hour, the judges had talked with all five girls. I descended to the basement and asked the judges if they had made a selection.

One judge told me, "No." They could not agree on a winner. Each had their selection and they could not find a way to resolve their difference. Neither intended to budge. *Politicians*, I thought. I had a problem on my hands. The meeting would be ending soon and the members were expecting to learn of the new Snow Queen. I did not care to be known thereafter as the guy who botched the Snow Queen Contest. I suggested to the judges that they find a way to come up with the winner. I asked them to be "imaginative," and said I would return in five minutes. When I returned there was no change. Action, I decided, was required. I took the judges aside and announced I was making an executive decision. I said I would flip a coin. If heads, the judge to my right would have the winner. Tails, the other judge. It was tails.

I went before the assembled membership and announced that Nadine was the new Snow Queen. I asked Nadine to come to the front of the room to receive her sweater. She was delighted by the award and full of joy. The members applauded. Ann, my former friend of many years, stood and pranced to the coatroom to collect her parka. With quick, sharp steps to punctuate her march to the door, she exited the building.

After the meeting, Nadine came up to me and planted one on my cheek. "Joe, that was so much fun. Thank you very much."

What could I say? I certainly could not have mentioned the flip of a coin.

"Nadine, you deserved it. There was no contestant better qualified to be Snow Queen."

Later in the evening, Ryan, the Club's president, found me at the rear of the room. He was displaying the same, strange smile he had the evening he appointed me Chairman of the contest.

"Joe, you did well."

I was not inclined to disagree.

"Thanks Ryan. It was an experience."

I could have added "education," but I kept that to myself.

As the crowd was thinning, Michael and I made our way to the bar. Together, we downed a few and discussed the evening's events before heading out into the chilly night air.

Henri Rochemont
(A creative nonfiction short story)

Henri asked me, in German, to please stop the vehicle. He said he had a pressing need to empty his bladder. As I brought the car to a halt along the right side of the highway, the headlights showed the road was elevated above the surrounding fields. It appeared there was a sudden drop-off on both sides of the road. Recalling as best I could the appropriate German words, I told him to be "careful" and that it was "low" out there. Maybe it was all that wine we had to drink. I was certain I had the correct words but I also realized that perhaps those words were not in Henri's German vocabulary. Whatever the cause, he failed to heed my cautions. He opened the car door, took one step and disappeared out of sight. Henri and I usually conversed in German since my French at that time was limited. Henri spoke no English, but he had learned German as a POW.

Concerned for my French friend, I stopped the engine, pulled the brake handle and hurried around the rear of the car. I hoped his injuries would be only minor. But as I peered down from the road's edge into the blackness below, his groans told me there was a problem of some degree. I hesitated from going any farther because I was hoping to avoid the same mistake Henri had made. After some delay, my friend started clawing his way up the bank. As he neared the top of the embankment I gave him a hand, helping him up to the last few steps. His right hand was bleeding and he kept rubbing his right ankle. After he relieved himself, I helped him into the car and we continued on our way.

Earlier in the day we had visited Henri's aging mother in Paris. He had told me he had not seen his mother in a while and a visit was long overdue. He had made me an offer. If I would drive him to Paris, he could promise me a fine home-cooked meal and some good wine to go with it. Since I had not experienced a home cooked meal in more than a year, Henri's offer was irresistible. To my great delight, the meal was everything he had promised. His mother was a gracious, quiet lady who lived alone in an apartment. She was delighted to see her son. After coffee we said our good-byes as we had several hours of driving to get home.

Once in the car, Henri suggested we might stop at a café that he had owned at one time. He said it would be only a little out of the way. "Sure," I said. When we arrived at the café, the proprietor greeted Henri with a friendly smile, a handshake and a hug. Henri introduced me as a friend and neighbor. The man was more than cordial to both of us. In a matter of minutes he sent the bartender for a good bottle of wine. While we were enjoying the drinks, the café's regular *fille du joie* walked over to our table. Henri knew her from past years and rose to give her a kiss on the cheek. Humming a tune he led her for a few whorls and dance steps in front of the bar. That was all! Neither of us was interested in a joy girl and Henri didn't wish to unnecessarily keep her away from prospects. When the bottle was empty, we said goodbyes again and were back on the road. To tell the truth, we didn't need the extra wine.

Henri was a neighbor of mine in Tours where I lived on Rue Lobin. We met one day while I was washing my car in the street. He did not have a car whereas I did. He knew some good fishing spots; I knew of none. I enjoyed fishing. So, we made a good match and a natural friendship developed. Occasionally we would get together to try our luck at some country stream. Sometimes we would bring along a young boy, Philippe, who Henri and his wife were boarding in their home.

Typically, when we would approach the fishing site, Henri would ask me, "Joseph, how about a coffee?" I always knew what he had in mind whether it was early morning or mid-afternoon. After we entered a café, the first thing he would ask the waitress was a question like, "What kind of house wine do you have today?"

Once in the café, there was never more talk about coffee. He always went for a full carafe of the lowest priced wine. To his way of thinking a varietal wine would be a waste of money. Both contained alcohol. He would take his time savoring the wine while I had a coffee or two. I enjoyed Henri's company. He was a free spirit and a good balance to my more serious nature. Henri explained to me that he learned German out of necessity as a prisoner of war. He was captured early in the war and was sent to work on a farm in Germany. The German farm girls taught him the language over a four-year period. On one of our fishing expeditions, Henri told me more about his German lessons.

"When I was on the farm, there were no men around. They were all off fighting somewhere. Once every several months a gestapo agent would come around to check on things. The women were longing for male companionship, and there I was. I was in demand.

"We, my girl friends and I, ate very well throughout the war—unlike many people in Germany. All of the crops did not go to the war effort. It was easy to hide ample food for everyone who lived on the farms. I would catch wild rabbits in the woods and trout in the streams. There were always chickens, eggs, potatoes and carrots. The vegetables could be hidden without difficulty. You merely dig a hole in the ground. Preferably one well away from the house. You put them in and cover them with dirt and leaves. They will keep that way until the spring. Now and then you go and retrieve whatever you need. In a way I was sorry to see the end of the war, and I believe the girls were disappointed to see me return to France."

When Henri and I finally arrived in Tours, I parked in the street near Henri's house. I had to help him out of the car and to the house. His ankle had grown to the size of a grapefruit, and he had difficulty leaning on that foot. At the front door, his wife was not pleased with the sight in front of her. Her husband, standing on one foot, was dirty and bloodied. He smelled of wine, his shirttail was half out. While her look accused me of multiple violations, she abstained from vocalizing her thoughts.

Henri was off his feet for a spell, but he did not seem to mind his predicament. The ankle gave him a good excuse for not going to work and, I am sure, for having a few extra glassfuls throughout the day.

Roisin

(A creative nonfiction short story)

After a meal of lamb and parsley potatoes, we remained at the dinner table while my aunt warmed water for tea. Uncle Peter lite a cigarette and, leaning back, told me, "I thought tomorrow we would visit your Aunt Roisin." I replied, "Sure, whatever you suggest." He took a draw on his smoke, hesitated and mused, "It's a bit of a drive, so I thought we would stay over a few days. Take our time."

I had travelled from an army base in France to visit my aunt and uncle in County Monaghan, Ireland. Mother had suggested that, since I was stationed not that far from Ireland, I might enjoy a visit with her brother and sister-in-law. When the weather warmed, I wrote to my uncle and he invited me for a stay.

After tea, Uncle Peter and I went to a pub in town where he intended to use the telephone there. He didn't yet have one at the house. At the pub, I went to the bar for a Guinness while Peter made arrangements with the proprietor to use the telephone that was in a back hallway. Peter went to make his call while I took a seat at the end of the bar. Two men were speaking in hushed tones at the other end of the bar. From where I sat I could hear Peter speaking with the operator. He placed the call and was promptly connected to Roisin. They chatted, apparently discussing our planned visit. I could hear some of what Peter was saying, but not all. Before hanging up, I distinctly heard him say, "Watch what you say." Strange, I thought, for a brother to say to a sister. At the time I gave no more thought to the comment, but the words long stuck in my memory. The significance of the caution didn't become known to me until decades later. When Peter came into the bar, he was surprised to see I had been sitting not far from the telephone he had been using.

Driving roads of the British Isles can be a challenge for an American. I had to continually concentrate on the task at hand in order to remain on the left side of the road. Turning corners in the towns is especially challenging. Except on the straight sections of the roads, I found it best to avoid becoming engaged in conversations. Roisin and her husband, Willie, heard us approach in the rental car and came out to welcome us. Peter did the introductions. In customary Irish tradition, we were invited to have ale or tea. I suggested tea.

Roisin and Willie lived in a small cottage near Lough Neagh, the largest lake in Great Britain. Their cottage reminded me of something out of a fairy tale. It was small, whitewashed top to bottom and had a thatched roof over all. Willie was employed by the RAF at a nearby military airfield. The couple had two small girls and two boys.

Roisin was everlastingly gracious and accommodating. She showed us to several sights around Northern Ireland and went out of her way to make special meals. The first evening, Roisin made a meal in my honor. She had bought a steak in town specifically for me and prepared it by boiling it in water. Others at the table ate chicken while I enjoyed the steak. One evening while Peter was telling a joke, I happened to turn and noticed Rosin studying me. She seemed lost in thought and her mind far away. I considered her gaze strange at the time, but gave the matter no more thought.

Rosin guided us farther north and to the Giant's Causeway, an unusual although natural collection of rocks along the western coastline. In Belfast we went to a museum that paid tribute to the RMS Titanic which was built at a local shipyard. In another museum we witnessed a number of artifacts that would be of primary interest to local Brits. A wing of one building displayed a chair upon which "…the queen sat while on her visit to Northern Ireland." I found the chair and its label amusing. Surely the queen had sat on more than one chair on her visit. How many other chairs had been enshrined? I was disinclined to comment. Brits, I learned, are sensitive to comments about their royals and quick to take umbrage with comments interpreted as bordering on disrespect.

On the second day, Roisin suggested she and I take a walk. She wanted to show me Lough Neagh which was close by. She said we could talk along the way. Willie and Peter would watch the house. She explained that the house was never unattended. To do so, if only for a brief time, might invite a flaming torch to the thatched roof. Two branches of Christianity were popular in the region although with theological differences important enough to warrant an action that might kill. As we made our way toward the lake, Roisin inquired about my life in the States. How's mother? Did we live in a house or an apartment? Was my brother also in the military? She was sincerely interested.

At the lake's edge we encountered a fisherwoman whom Rosin seemed to know. After the two exchanged greetings, Roisin asked if the woman had "any luck" that day. She responded, "Oh, yes. Would you like to see it?" Roisin looked to me. I said, "Sure."

We were led along the lakeshore to a nearby shack and to a box inside the size of a steamer truck. When the woman lifted the lid, dozens of agitated ells suddenly began churning around and under one another. Their eyes seemed to watch their tormentors. The sudden appearance of the slimy, snake-like creatures caused me to step back. I asked what the woman intended to do with her catch. "Oh," she said, "I ship them to London. Ells are very popular over there."

Rosin bought an ell from her neighbor and carried it back to the house. When she served the fish on a platter that evening, the pieces were still twitching. It seemed I was the only diner surprised by an entrée that was still moving about.

On the third day "up north" it was time to return south again. Then people in Ireland and Northern Ireland didn't hug one another the way Americans do today, but Roisin sincerely wished me well. We said our goodbyes before Peter and I headed south. It was the last time I saw Roisin although we occasionally exchanged letters in later years.

During the reminder of my stay, Peter continued showing me around and introducing me to "friends." In Irish speak, friends are relatives. I never learned what the Irish call those people I would call friends. The Irish friends all tried their best to fill me with tea or beer and good cheer. One day we went to a Gaelic game, a serious and ancient Irish game that seemed a mix of rugby and soccer. The competitors sometimes killed one another with their enthusiasm and high kicks. Eventually I had to return to camp in France. I considered my stay in the British Isles an opportunity to experience a way of life very different from the one I knew in America. My time in Ireland also showed me the kind of life my mother had for the nineteen years she lived there prior to her emigrating.

When I returned to the States and civilian life, my parents were anxious to hear of my experiences overseas. Mother, in particular, questioned me about the brothers and sisters she hadn't seen since leaving Ireland many years in the past. I mentioned my stay with Roisin in Northern Ireland, but I thought mother was not especially interested in hearing about that particular visit. In general, I noticed, mother was disinclined to discuss her days in Ireland.

The years ticked by and years turned into decades. In time, I am sorry to say, both Peter and Roisin passed away. First Peter, then Roisin. Also, both my parents. I miss them all to this day.

A year ago, an envelope came to me in the mail. It was postmarked San Francisco, although I grew to doubt it originated in California. The note inside was brief. All that was written was: "Roisin is your sister."

The writer hadn't signed the note. Strange, I thought. Who would send such a peculiar message? Although skeptical, I wondered if there was any truth to the peculiar note. Despite the pretenses of relatives, could it be that Roisin was actually my sister, half-sister to be exact? In an effort to solve the mystery I called cousin Macartin in Ireland and asked him directly. After a hesitation, he confirmed that, yes, it was true. Roisin was my sister.

Making additional inquiries after speaking with Macartin, I learned that as a teenager, mother was impregnated by a local farm boy. Her father insisted she marry the boy, but mother didn't want to be married to the lad as well as, so to speak, his farm. Mother chose to emigrate to America and, alone, bravely crossed the Atlantic. To start a new life in a country full of strangers – away from hidden whispers and innuendos. It was a different era.

I sometimes find myself thinking of Roisin. My parents likewise. I wonder if my father knew about Roisin. Back then a groom expected his bride to be a virgin. And why did the relatives think it so important to hide the truth for so many decades. I would have enjoyed talking with Roisin as a brother rather than as a respectful nephew. I would have kidded her about something in the British way of life. I would have used the term "Limy." With devilment in her eye, she would have placed a hand on my arm and called me a "Yank." We would have had a good laugh.

Camping with Friends
(A fictional short story)

Melvin and I both worked for a firm that developed computer programs. That was before the pandemic and the mass layoffs that ensued. Melvin was the janitor in the building; I was a programmer. Back then, neither of us found either the time or the interest in speaking to the other. We each had our own set of peers as well as tasks to be addressed. There was, however, one day Melvin and I spoke albeit briefly. I happened to be in the men's room when he was tending plumbing in one of the stools. He happened to see me nearby and turned to say, "Damn guys. They piss on the seats; too lazy to lift a seat. Where do they find these characters?" All I said was, "Who knows. Characters are everywhere." That was the extent of our conversation until years later when the evolution of events cast us together in a common need to survive.

Our employer gave Melvin and me notice the same day. The human resources people herded some fifty of us into a large cavernous room. They were decent about the occasion. I'll give them credit for putting on a good front. The chief Human Resources honcho made a little speech preliminary to the big punch. He said management was "sorry" and truly projected genuine regret. Strange, I thought, how he did that. Reflecting on the firing, I often wondered if HR people practice saying how sorry they are for the things they do. At home, do they individually stand before a mirror to test their delivery? Do they meet periodically to practice and test one another? Oh, Linda, try looking sad the whole time you are making your good-by speech. That smile near the end is inconsistent with what we want to project. We need to make employees think we really mean it when we say we are sorry for giving them the boot. Keep smiles for when we are attracting people to the company not when we want to get rid of them. Let's try that again.

While I was eligible for unemployment checks, I went regularly to the unemployment office. In their facility the state offered listings of job openings and other literature free for the taking. Sometimes the unemployment people wanted to talk. Mostly, I determined, they wanted to be sure I was looking for another job. I suppose management had given them their mandates: Make sure these people are trying to find work. We don't want to send out unemployment checks any more than necessary. Several times I saw Melvin there. We recognized one another and exchanged "hellos" on occasion. I would call Melvin an uncomplicated type. I learned later he had dropped out of high school. Because he had a lisp, the other kids made fun of him. He merely wanted to get away from the people who were constantly making fun of him. He told me he regretted having the lisp, but he could do nothing about it. Despite his limited education, Melvin was nobody's fool. He followed the national and international news with keen interest and was well abreast of the ongoing issues in Washington. Several weeks before the checks were due to run out, we discussed our dilemma in detail and with some urgency.

Melvin and I both gradually came to the same, disappointing conclusion: We would both be unable to afford the rent for our respective apartments once the unemployment checks stopped showing up in our mailboxes. That was when I told Melvin of my intention to move into a tent far east of town. I told him I owned this eight foot wall tent that my ex and I had used on camping trips, and I was going to go camping full time. I said that I had enough money saved to pay for a camping site and food well into the future. I said I thought I had no choice. I was not going to live in the streets with dangerous and unkempt homeless people. I added that I wanted a place with clean bathrooms and showers. My camping plans caught

Melvin's attention. He asked a few questions, and I could see he was becoming seriously interested in my game plan.

The next time I saw Melvin at the unemployment office he seemed unusually pleased to see me. He smiled when he saw me which was in contrast with his normal dour demeanor. After a few pleasantries, he told me he liked my camping plans and, in fact, had priced a tent. Events developed rapidly from that time on. Two weeks later, Melvin and I packed up what few possessions we could keep in a tent. I left my furniture and other belongings for the landlord. I figured that to some extent he could use the items as part payment toward the rents I hadn't paid the last few months. I didn't know what Melvin did with his belongings. Sometimes it's best to avoid asking too many personal questions. I'll say this: Everything he brought fit easily into the trunk of my car. Melvin didn't own a car, so I volunteered to drive him and his gear to the campground. The drive east and up into the mountains took ninety minutes. We arrived on a beautiful, sunny day in July. In the distance I could see snow-capped mountains. Those mountains were beautiful to behold, but the snow served to remind us cold weather would arrive one day. I negotiated a good rate at the campground. I explained to the owner that we needed two sites and, in addition, we were planning on staying long-term.

I took a site near the bathrooms, the showers and the front office. If I had to go in the middle of the night, I didn't want to be stumbling along a muddy path and tripping over tree roots. Melvin said he liked the calmness of the woods and selected a spot at the rear of the property. It was just as well that our tents were separated by a good distance. If we were side-by-side, we might soon grow tired of one another's company.

Our first evening at the campground, Melvin came over to my new quarters. I had brought two kitchen chairs with me from my apartment: One for the occasional guest and one for me. Although the confines of the tent allowed little room for possessions, I considered two substantial chairs a necessity. I opened a bottle of pinot noir from my collection, and we toasted our new way of life. The wine seemed to loosen Melvin's tongue. He became uncharacteristically talkative. He told me he was the youngest of three children. His mother raised her brood after his father left the house one night and didn't come back. He spoke lovingly of his mother and I noticed a tear appear in the corner of his eye. Melvin was a good conversationalist. He read all kinds of periodicals and books and could speak knowingly on a range of subjects. Unlike most of my former co-workers, he didn't try to impress with tales of accomplishment or his sundry collection of wonderful possessions. He showed sincere interest in other people's opinions and aspirations. Being a former janitor, he also displayed a mechanically inclination. He noticed what he called problems with the drainage around the outside of my tent and made certain corrections. He explained that the way I had the drainage arranged I would have most certainly experienced wet feet at the first rain.

Melvin and I settled into the routine of life in a campground. I would have a granola bar and water for breakfast. I skipped lunch because it was too much trouble finding and preparing something to eat. Most mornings I would go for a walk in the hills behind the campground. I had always enjoyed hiking and taking in nature's scenery. Often I saw wildlife on my treks. All kinds of songbirds, deer. One morning I saw a weasel scurry after a wood rat. Skunks, too. Since our arrival at the campground, the weather had been nothing but wonderful. The dry and crisp air of the mountains lifted the spirit. Of course, we both knew staying warm during the coming cold weather would be a challenge. We both agreed we would worry about that particular challenge at a later day. Perhaps we both secretly thought and hoped that in time we might find an alternative to living in a tent in cold weather.

In our new way of life, Melvin and I didn't find many pleasures in our new life. Nevertheless, we decided eating well would be one of them. Much to my surprise, Melvin and I became good friends. More than anything, our friendship was based on a common need to survive without a regular source of income. I already owned a two-burner Coleman camp stove. Melvin bought a single burner. He said that if he needed a second burner, then he would buy another one-burner. In the evenings both Melvin and I prepared a cooked meal. I usually made a trip to the valley every two or three days to buy groceries. We had no way to keep food other than canned goods, but neither of us used canned food that much. On each trip to the valley I bought only what we needed for the next two or three days. Once a week, we would get together for a meal with a special entrée. One week, Melvin would make a meal for two at his tent, the next week would be my turn. The guest cook would provide a bottle of wine; that was the rule. On occasion, we would invite another resident of the campground for supper. Despite our limited means, we both consistently made meals that were both appetizing and nutritious.

After several of our get-togethers, I started to wonder about Melvin's sexual orientation. Unlike heterosexual man I had ever known, he never mentioned women. Some men, I learned, are more explicit with friends than others, quick to talk about fast women, one night stands or special conquests of the past. Other men will mention wives or former girlfriends in a more courtly manner. Nevertheless, most men are inclined to eventually discuss women and sex. To compare notes so to speak. It's in the male DNA. Not so with Melvin. Although I tried to gingerly broach the subject, he didn't seem inclined to respond. He never suggested that he thought about women to any degree. Could it be that he was gay? Or merely asexual? The love he declared for this mother seemed characteristic of a homo. Whatever his bent, I concluded I would avoid further mention of women to him. In our present prediction we both needed a trustworthy and reliable companion. I thought that my mentioning his avoidance of the subject might engender animosity or resentment.

In time, Melvin and I both met other people at the campground. A few were typical campers - people we envied, people with employment and a house elsewhere. Those types stayed at the campground a mere few days or a week before departing. Melvin and I would say a friendly "hello" but otherwise didn't bother to engage transients in conversation. A few of the newcomers to the campground had given up their comfortable places of abode due to necessity and, much as Melvin and I, came to the conclusion that life in a campground was an acceptable alternative to other dreadful options. Some continued to stew in the gloom of their bad luck and stayed to themselves. We avoided those types.

One day Melvin told me a middle aged woman moved into the campground near his stand. To make her acquaintance, I walked to her tent and introduced myself. She told me she was also from the West Coast. She had been a graphics designer before she was terminated. She was attractive with long black hair and dark brown eyes. Somewhat business-like and prissy. Said her name was Regina. We chatted a few minutes and, to my surprise, she asked if there was a shooting range nearby. I suspected her purpose was to advertise that she could ably protect herself and with deadly force if need be. I told Regina I didn't know of a shooting range, but I told her to simply go in the woods behind the campground and do her practice there. Find a big tree and let it have it. I told her Melvin and I were having beef bourguignon at my place that Friday and she was welcome. I told her we would consider the event her welcoming party. That brought a smile, and she seemed delighted at the invitation. She said she would be over and asked if she should bring anything. I told her "No, just yourself."

For Regina's welcoming party, I borrowed a third chair so that the three of us could sit when we ate and, perhaps, drank. Regina was early for dinner and brought along a fresh gallon of Gallo mountain burgundy. We started on the wine well before the beef was ready. By dinnertime we had big appetites. I received numerous compliments on my cooking. After dinner, we had more wine. What the hell, none of us had any place to go to other than our lonely tents. Conversation came easily as the wine flowed. We compared notes on the campground and, the concern in the back of our minds, how to cope with the coming cold weather. I volunteered that having ample wine handy would help. Regina became nostalgic talking about a boyfriend she had only the prior year. A boyfriend who disappeared into the fog. She could show a sharp edge at times. When talking about her last employer, she peppered her speech with words as "bastards," "mothers," and "child molesters." I told Regina I had no such feeling toward my past employer. Business was business and "those people" did what they had to do in their everlasting quest to make a buck. I said I held out hope my last employer would call me back some day.

The day after the party, I stayed mostly on my cot. A wine hangover is the worst kind. I had a lingering headache and nausea throughout the day. By midnight I had a slight appetite, but I didn't eat anyway. The following day I was up and about although still walking gingerly. I drove down to McDonald's in the valley and ordered a hamburger for breakfast – my first hamburger in five years. Afterward, I went for a drive to tour the roads in the area. That afternoon, I walked over to Melvin's tent. The flap on the tent was open because it was a hot day. Melvin was reclined on his cot, and initially I turned to leave as I didn't wish to wake him. Apparently he was not sleeping and he called to me, "Don't go. I was going to pay you a visit anyway." He added the obvious: "I think we had too much wine the other night. Next time I'm going to have to keep score better. It was Regina's fault. I'm blaming our hangovers on her." Melvin stood and walked to the corner of his tent where he had a case of wine. He withdrew a bottle of a California Chardonnay and worked the cork loose. He handed me a paper cup with the wine and told me, "This will make you feel better."

The onset of cooler weather prompted me to consider some kind of heat for my tent. I discussed my problem with the owner of the campground who suggested a coal-burning camp stove. He explained wood stoves are cheaper than wood stoves and wood can be obtained free, but a coal fire lasts longer. With wood, a person must tend to the fire at least once or twice during a cold night. On the other hand, a coal fire will last throughout the night. I told both Regina and Melvin I was going to order a coal-burning stove. Both asked me to also order one for them; I did although I didn't think either would actually pay me. Time proved me correct. Melvin, handyman that he was, modified all three tent roofs to accommodate stove pipes.

Regina kept busy chilly days drawing in her tent, practicing at a genuine talent. Melvin was into crossword puzzles, jig puzzles and books. Mostly, I read. Melvin also retrofitted all three tents with windows so that we had adequate light inside our tents for whatever we wanted to see or do. Regina said she wanted to be part of our weekly cook fest, so we made our club a club of three. Time proved her the best of the three cooks. Once she had two glasses of wine, she loosened up and in fact became entertaining. Her repertoire of jokes was both surprising and entertaining.

The campground had a heated rec room with a TV and hi-fi. When the cold weather and snow arrived, the three of us spent most winter days within the confines of that room. On occasion, I noticed each of my companions starring out at the snow, thinking or daydreaming. I often wondered if they were each thinking of certain pleasant days of the past, days when they each had employment, friends and a place they called home. Or was it their current dilemma that caused their minds to wander? I, too, caught myself looking out those windows and concentrating on the snow for long periods. At night the rec room was closed to all, and then we were obliged to return to our tents.

Little Pietro
(A fiction short story)

After having worked for many years, I retired a year ago. I had very much been looking forward to retirement as employment the last few years was not all that satisfying. I had found myself obligated to deal with disagreeable people while spending time on boring projects. In addition, I had to travel long distances after the office had moved. To do so, I had to arise around five-thirty every morning. I did it for years. When the day of retirement arrived, I was more than pleased to call it quits.

I readily settled into the life of a retiree. I started reading books that for years had been on my to-do list. My wife and I ate out frequently. We visited friends. I started going to the gym more. Most of all, I relished sleeping in late in the mornings. I would go to bed around midnight. In the mornings I would sleep until I didn't feel like sleeping anymore. Some evenings I would set the alarm for five-thirty although I had no plans to go anywhere the following day. In the morning I would shut the alarm off, tell myself how great it was to sleep-in and go back to sleep. Most mornings I was up by eight. I was enjoying the life of a retiree—until the chickens showed up in my yard. Everything changed that day.

Ann, my wife, and I were returning home after eating lunch at a local diner. As I turned to pull into the driveway to our house, I spotted the chickens. There were five of them. When I first saw them, I commented to Ann, "Aren't those chickens in our front yard? I can't imagine where they came from."

The birds in my front yard were walking around looking for things to eat in the grass, pecking here and there. They were not going in any particular direction. After I parked the car in the garage, I walked over to where the chickens were meandering about. I was curious and wanted to get a better look at these unusual intruders. The two roosters, I must admit, were handsome creatures. They each had black tail feathers that rose up from their rumps in an arc, and they sported a variety of colors. They acted proud of their garish outfit. The hens, on the other hand, were of more muted colors. The hens seemed pragmatic as they went about their business. They didn't seem as egotistical as the roosters. When I drew near I noticed the birds were not full sized chickens. Although they seemed full-grown, they were small—like midget chickens.

At first, the chickens ignored me as they walked about, heads bobbing down now and then for something to eat. I came closer, and they gradually changed their courses to keep a distance from me. When I ran after them, they scurried off. They didn't trust me. One of the hens dropped a do-do as it fled in what seemed to be in the spirit of, "Here's to you, buster." I went in the house, hoping the invaders would vanish.

When the next morning came around, I knew the chickens were nearby. Around five-thirty, I heard the first "cock-a-doodle-do." My eyes snapped open, and I found myself staring at the ceiling. In suburban developments, one does not expect chickens calling to announce the arrival of dawn. For the better part of the next hour, the noise continued. Both Ann and I decided to eat breakfast three hours earlier than when we would normally eat. Once in the kitchen, I looked out the window in an effort to spot the inconsiderate source of the noise. I didn't see the chickens, but I spotted a box that I hadn't seen before in the backyard of my neighbor, Mario Calversi.

I returned to the kitchen table, grabbed a piece of toast, smeared butter on it and returned to the window for another look. After I swallowed a piece of toast, I told Ann, "I think I know where the chickens came from."

Surprised, Ann said, "Where?"

I told her, "Mario has a chicken coop in his back yard."

"You're kidding."

I told her, "Would I kid over something as serious as this?"

In the following days, the chickens continued coming into my yard. I noticed they liked earth worms, but they also went after any insect that moved. They relished grass hoppers and were quick to fight over grass hoppers. Mario, I noticed, put out corn for his chickens, but that didn't seem to be enough for them. They spent half the day looking for more things to eat. The first week or two I enjoyed to some extent watching the little chickens. They always stayed together as a group. Of the two roosters, I noticed one was larger than the other. The larger bird considered itself to be boss and the hens its harem. It would not let the other rooster near the hens. If the smaller rooster came near one of the hens, the boss would chase him off. On occasion, the two rosters would spar, but the fights never lasted more than a few seconds. The boss rooster had serious-looking spurs and he was quick to use them on what it considered the competition. The smaller rooster inevitably gave up the fights and moved off a short distance.

For some reason, the chickens liked lounging on my deck. After they became tired of searching the grass for things, they would fly up to the rail of my deck. Some days they would stay there for hours at a time. Periodically the boss rooster would copulate with one of the hens. The rooster had amazing stamina! It would be doing duty from early morning until sundown. The lesser rooster would watch from a distance, no doubt hoping for its day.

The chickens always left behind deposits on my deck. Before I could sit there, I would drag the hose from the garage and squirt the stuff into the grass. Every evening the birds would wander to the small coop in Mario's back yard. They wanted to be home before the sun went down.

Both Ann and I would arise with the cock's crow. We would have our breakfast, read the paper and…wait. After about an hour, the roosters grew quiet and we would return to bed for another two or three hours of sleep. This became our daily routine. In time, I considered speaking to Mario about the chickens. I felt a *tête-à-tête* was in the offing.

I had always preferred to avoid confrontations with neighbors of any description. Once started, there is no predicting where a confrontation might end. I learned Mario had an attitude. If a branch from one of my shrubs came over the property line by an inch, he would be quick to cut it off. Then he would throw it back in my yard. I don't know why! He acted as though he considered the twig some kind of an evil intrusion. An insult! A lack of proper respect! With Mario, I followed the rule of thumb: The more you stirred a turd, the more it stunk. I didn't like stink. Above all, I tried to avoid him and stink.

Before I was to go head-to-head with my neighbor, I thought I would try the legal approach. Let somebody other than me do the heavy lifting. I went to the township hall to inquire about the rules. They had rules for just about everything: curb size, building setback, noise, maximum grass height. Maybe they had one about chickens. At the township hall, a young woman behind a desk asked me, "What can I do for you?"

I told her, "I have a problem with a neighbor."

"What kind of a problem?"

"He's raising livestock in his backyard. I didn't think our neighborhood was zoned farming."

She asked, "What kind of livestock? Where do you live?"

"Chickens."

I told her my address.

"You're right, chickens are not allowed in your neighborhood."

I was pleased with what she told me. I thought I would be a winner after all. Then, she asked, "What kind of chickens? Are they regular chickens or bantams?"

I told her, "I thought chickens were chickens."

She hesitated, and then told me the bad news.

"Full sized chickens are considered livestock. People raise full sized chickens either for the eggs or because they intend to eat them. Bantams are considered pets and are usually not eaten. In other words, bantams are not considered livestock. They are allowed. We've been through this with other people in the past."

The air went out of my sail.

The bantams continued the morning reveilles, visiting my yard and my deck. Why they never went to the neighbor's yard on the other side of Mario's, I'll never understand. After the passage of more time, I decided it was truly time for the needed *tête-à-tête*. Rules of thumb or no rules of thumb, I was becoming perturbed. The next time I saw Mario, he was in his backyard, throwing corn to the chickens. I walked over, trying to avoid stepping in the chicken shit that was just about everywhere. When he turned, I asked, "Hey, Mario, I see you have some chickens."

"Yeah, my brother-in-law gave them to me."

He hesitated before going on.

"They're not called chickens though. They're bantams."

Mario, I could see, wanted to be one step ahead of me. I thought diplomacy might work best with Mario. Trying to avoid being direct, I asked, "You going to keep them?"

He didn't answer me. Instead, he told me, "The big rooster's name is Little Pietro. Anyway, that's what my brother-in-law called him."

I was wondering why the Italian name. I asked, "Is he Italian too?" Then I added, "I mean your brother-in-law."

Mario looked at me but declined as answer. Maybe I was getting too personal. I decided to return to the chickens. I asked him, "That's an unusual name. Do the other chickens have names?"

"No, I don't think Sal named the others."

The chicken's names were the least of my problems, so I abandoned the subject. I was inclined to give Mario a piece of my mind, but, at the same time, I thought any expression of my true feelings would only make matters worse. Maybe he would retaliate by getting more chickens. I had to devise another plan, but not at that moment. It was time for me to go, so I thought I would say something stupid as I left.

As I turned to leave, I told Mario, "I was just wondering."

I think it was two days after I talked with Mario. I was sitting on the deck reading a paperback. Ann was in the kitchen baking something. The chickens, or bantams if you will, were a little below me in the backyard, doing what they usually did. In the corner of my eye I noticed a shadow pass over the deck. At first, I thought it was another vulture. Vultures often pass over the house, and sometimes only a few feet above the roof. However, this time it wasn't a vulture. When I looked up, I could see it was a red-tailed hawk, otherwise commonly known as a "chicken hawk."

The hawk flew off a short distance and then returned. It started circling above my yard, considering its next meal. I told myself *There is a God and He sent this bird to me.* To avoid scaring the winged predator away, I hunched over and crept to the sliding door. Slowly I disappeared inside the house. Please, I whispered, "Let it be Little Pietro."

The next time I saw the fowl there was one less hen. "Damn." I spoke out loud as I looked out the kitchen window. That time Ann heard me talking to myself, and she asked what was wrong. I told her a chicken hawk probably took one of the hens. "Aw," she said, "that's too bad." I wondered whose side she favored. Or, was she disappointed that the hawk had chosen a female instead of a male, forget the fact that it was the males that were the major source of the problem. I also wondered if there was some way I could draw more hawks to our property. Was there such a thing as a hawk call?

I stayed away from the deck, but the hawk didn't return. Maybe it preferred the taste of rabbits or squirrels to bantams. Who Knows? I told Mario about the hawk. I didn't want him contemplating revenge. According to the *Godfather* movie, Italians can be quick to go to revenge, and they can be imaginative. To my surprise, Mario already knew about the hawk. He told me he found the hen's bones and feathers under the tall oak tree at the rear of his backyard. Apparently the hawk didn't take its prey far away before dining. Maybe it was truly hungry that day.

Ann and I continued with our daily routine. Up early, eat breakfast, read the paper, back to bed until nine. Later in the day, I would hose the deck. This went on for a month after the hawk paid us a visit. I was at a loss for ideas. Then, it occurred to me. Why not kidnap Little Pietro? I wouldn't kill the little rascal, although it would be a pleasure to do so. I would take him out to where there are farms and turn him loose. The rooster would miss his free food and free sex, but what the hell. It's already had more than its fair share of both. Rooster number two would love me. I would deal with number two another day and in another way.

I secretly started making plans for the kidnapping. I didn't want Mario to know I stole one of his bantams. I didn't want consequences. No, I had to do it so that Mario would think the hawk took another of his little darlings. I would throw a few feathers in his yard to suggest another hawk attack. I bought some cracked corn at a feed mill, and I started feeding the bantams. I wanted them to trust me so that I could get near them. If Mario saw me feeding the birds, he would think I didn't mind them and, in fact, had grown to like his diminutive pets.

I decided the kidnapping would take place when Mario and his wife were away from their house. In the past, Mario let it be known he followed the local baseball team. He said he was an enthusiastic fan. I started checking the team's weekend schedule. One Saturday afternoon when I thought Mario might go to a game, I began watching out the dining room window. I thought that if Mario were going to the game, he would depart his house about an hour before the game. Sure enough, I spotted Mario and his wife entering their car. He was wearing a baseball cap and she a sun bonnet. They were going to the game.

I went to my basement where I had the net at the ready for the occasion. It was similar to a butterfly net only larger with a long handle. I chased the bantams from the deck and they flew down to the backyard. I followed and began throwing corn in front of me. They weren't interested. I guess they had already eaten. No problem. With net elevated, I walked slowly toward the birds. They moved away, keeping suspicious eyes on me. In a burst of speed, I went directly for Little Pietro. It was now or never. Unfortunately, I learned the little guy could fly faster than I could run.

Back in the house, I was obliged to explain the strange-looking net as well as defeat to Ann. She was not sympathetic. I was resigned again to the daily routine imposed upon us by circumstances. I saw no alternative.

It was several weeks after my failed kidnapping attempt. I automatically woke up at the usual five-thirty, expecting the usual avian reveille. But, there was none. Ann, too, climbed out of bed. Together and puzzled, we headed for the kitchen and breakfast. When I looked toward Mario's property, I didn't see the bantams anywhere. Then, I noticed their coop was missing. Later that day I saw Mario and I asked about the bantams. I tried to avoid displaying my delight. He told me, "I returned them to my brother-in-law. Maria said their crowing kept her from sleeping. And, there was the mess in the yard. The bantams will be more at home at Sal's. He has a little farm out in the country."

I told Ann the good news. All she said was, "We can start sleeping late again."

The Yazidis
(A fictional short story)

Kathryn and I were having our usual evening cocktails when I made the announcement.

"Kathryn, it's been a great run. But the time has come. We have no one to take over the business, and we have enough investments to last us as long as we live. I'm going to sell the business."

I didn't know how Kathryn would react. She stopped sipping her drink and held her martini up high.

"I'll drink to that. Why did you wait so long?"

I had been running the dealership since the day I inherited it from dad years ago. On dad's last day he told me, "Do what you can." I never figured out exactly what dad intended. Maybe he thought I was not up to his level when it came to business. He might have been right on that score, but McGroder Motors gave Kathryn and me a decent income over the years. No complaints there.

I made some inquiries, and within a month I found a buyer for the business. After settlement, Kathryn and I settled into the life of retirees. As the months ticked by though, we found we had more time than things to do. We started watching TV more than we had previously. One evening we were in the family room watching the news—as had become our custom. The anchor man was talking about the turmoil the ISIS fanatics in

Syria and Iraq were stirring up. He reported the terrorists were pursuing the followers of an ancient religion known as the Yazidis. Although I couldn't see Kathryn from behind my Wall Street Journal, I had no difficulty hearing her.

"Isn't that terrible? Those Islamic radicals killing all those people. Just because they have a different belief. Cutting off heads, burning people alive. Terrible, just terrible. What savages."

I had to agree. It was a terrible development. I set my Journal aside for a moment and started listening to the TV commentator. The man continued talking about the plight of the Yazidis. Those people, he explained, had fled their homes for fear of being murdered and were living who knows where. Men, women, families, old people, children. They had little food, water or shelter. The news broadcast came to an end and I returned to my Journal. I was always on the lookout for news about any of the stocks I owned.

The following evening at supper Kathryn looked at me over her plate of lasagna and broccoli. She sat her fork aside and reached for her glass of Burgundy.

"Last night I kept thinking of all those poor people stranded on that mountain. I couldn't get them out of my thoughts. There must be children amongst those people. What an unfortunate, hopeless people. Fanatics in the distance bent on killing them."

I could see it was the motherly instinct kicking in. Children in peril will do that to a woman.

I told Kathryn, "Yes, that certainly is a terrible plight for those unfortunate people."

After a few sips of wine Kathryn looked at me again.

"Do you think there is a way we could help those people? What I mean is: We have this big house. You said we have more money than we could ever use. Do you think there's a way we could be of assistance?"

I had to admit: Kathryn had a point. Where was the compassion? She and I have been leading a life of ease. Perhaps it was time to think of the less fortunate. Kathryn's concern was more or less the basis for the start of our peculiar adventure. We decided it was time to act!

The day after we heard about the Yazidis I called the Department of State in Washington and asked for the telephone number of the American Embassy in Baghdad. I was given a number and when I placed the call a woman answered.

"American Embassy, Baghdad. May I be of assistance?"

As I could not detect an accent I assumed she was American. Actually, I thought she might be from down South somewhere. Maybe Alabama. When I was in the army I dated a girl from Alabama. Loved that accent.

"Yes. I am calling from the United States. My wife and I have been following the plight of the Yazidi people over there and we thought we would like to help."

"One moment, sir. I will connect you with an assistant to the ambassador."

Music stated sounding in the receiver. Russian music of all things! At an American embassy. Minutes went by. Followed by more minutes. Eventually a man spoke.

"Hello, this is Mason Baxter."

"Good morning, sir. My name is Kevin McGroder. My wife and I have been hearing about the plight of those unfortunate Yazidi people stuck up there in the mountains north of Baghdad. We would like to help if we may. I mean financially. That is what I meant to say."

Hearing my actual, spoken words convinced me that Kathryn and I were doing what was called for. I became pleased with myself and more determined than before to pursue this matter. To help some desperate people. The original thought was Kathryn's and, I had to admit, she deserved the credit. I momentarily became entangled in my thoughts to the extent that the return of Mason Baxter's voice startled me.

"That is kind of you, sir, but, frankly, I know of no way that we at the embassy could be of assistance. An effort of that type would take a lot of coordination and financing. We have only limited resources at this embassy. We are all very busy, as you might suspect. Besides, everything we do must be strictly along official lines. What you are suggesting is not the sort of thing we normally become involved with. I am sorry."

"That's too bad. We were hoping to be of assistance to the Yazidis. You know, by directly helping a couple with children who are in need of food and shelter. My wife and I were thinking that perhaps we could find a deserving family and pay for their transportation to America. We have a big house and we could put them up for a spell. We have the money if something can be worked-out."

Mr. Baxter was silent. I think the mention of money caught his attention. I waited, but I heard nothing.

"Mr. Baxter, are you still there?"

"Sorry, sir. I was just thinking."

In the background I could hear a variety of sounds including people speaking. Perhaps a printer cranking out paper at a high speed. Mr. Baxter hesitated, possibly waiting for the sounds to abate. When he spoke again his voice was lowered, and it sounded as though he might have his hand cupped over the handset.

"Possibly something could be done. You say you would be interested in helping. Financially, I mean. That is, to assist a needy couple?"

"Yes, that is what I had in mind. We were thinking more of the children."

"If you would give me your name and phone number I will give consideration to your request. Maybe this could be handled unofficially, outside the embassy if you know what I mean."

"Good. My name is Kevin McGroder."

I gave him my telephone number. In response he told me, "Mr. McGroder, the transportation costs you are suggesting would be in the thousands of dollars. Are you prepared to go forward with expenses of that size?"

"My wife and I don't have unlimited funds, but, yes, that is what we had in mind. Something along those lines."

"Fair enough. I will make some inquiries and call you back in a day or two. If that would be alright with you?"

"Yes, please see what you can do, and call me when you have something in mind. Or, for that matter, call anytime you wish."

I suspected that Mr. Baxter figured he would be entitled to a little compensation for his trouble. I didn't mind—if that is what would be required to make it all happen. I did not have a list of other prospects that could make this project take place. After I hung up, I told myself, "Yes, this was a wonderful idea that Kathryn had."

I knew Kathryn would be pleased to hear the news.

Three days after my call to Baghdad the telephone rang at six in the morning. It was Mr. Baxter, and he was speaking in a more audible voice. He advised me that he found a needy family. He said that he estimated the driver fees and airline fares to transport a man, a woman and two children to the USA would total around $8,000. He added he would be doing the arrangements on his own time and not officially through the embassy. So, he said, the check should be made payable to him. I wired the requested funds to him later that day. Two weeks later Kathryn and I headed to the airport to meet four refugees: a man, a woman and two small girls.

On the way to the airport Kathryn was full of talk. She asked questions out loud, speaking to no one in particular. I detected doubts and anxiety in her speach. Do you think we are doing the right thing? I hope they will like it in America. Let's hope they are clean people. Mr. Baxter had told me little about the refugees. He said the man was of medium height and slender. The woman was also slender and of average height. The girls were 10 and 13. Otherwise we knew next to nothing of the family. At the airport we had no trouble spotting the newcomers. The four seemed bewildered as they walked from the airplane toward the immigration area, looking left and right. The sights and sounds must have seemed strange to them. The man led the way while the woman followed with the girls. She carried a small valise. His hands were free at his side. The immigration agent viewed and stamped their passports. On the American side of customs the man saw the sign with my name and he walked up to me. The other three followed although at a distance.

"Mr. McGroder, I am Vian Khalif."

"Welcome to America, Mr. Khalif."

We shook hands.

"Sir, I am most grateful for you kindness. I doubt that I will ever be able to repay you for your kind generosity. I believe you are aware that we are destitute. We have nothing."

I was surprised to learn the man spoke English surprisingly well. His enunciations were distinctly American and not British. His hand shake, posture and confidence indicated he was not from a background of manual labor. The woman and the children remained silent and did not seem obligated to speak with either Kathryn or me. I thought I should introduce Mr. Khalid to Kathryn. It seemed the appropriate thing to do.

"Mr. Khalif, this is my wife, Kathryn."

I was uncertain as to how the introduction would go. Men from the Mideast relate differently to women than men from the West. Vian, I learned, conducted himself as a professional diplomat.

"How do you do, Mrs. McGroder? I am pleased to meet you."

He bowed forward slightly, smiling pleasantly. Kathryn told him, "welcome." We stood silent for a spell while, it seemed, Kathryn expected some mention of the woman who was standing a few feet away. But, it didn't happen. I learned later the woman's name was Narin, but Mr. Khalif made no mention of her or the children. I concluded we had enough introductions for the time being and it was time to move on.

We took the newcomers to our house in a van I had rented for the occasion. Vian rode up front with me while Kathryn rode in the back with Narin and the two girls. It was a seating arrangement we had decided upon on our way to the airport. Vian sat with his forearms on his lap the entire trip. He was continually looking out the window much as a wonderstruck child at Christmas. He spoke only in the way of an answer if I asked him a question. Always with deference. Nobody in the back was speaking.

Kathryn and I had decided the Khalifs would live upstairs in our house where we had several bedrooms and two bathrooms. Once home, we showed the guests to their new quarters. Kathryn and I retreated to our kitchen on the first floor. Taking a seat at the table, Kathryn asked me, "What do you think?"

I told her, "I don't know. To be sure they have different ways. I didn't hear the woman or the girls utter a peep. I guess they are taught to be that way. You know, part of their culture. Speak only when spoken to."

Kathryn blinked her eyes a few times but said nothing. She was unsmiling. I secretly hoped she was not disappointed with our guests and the beginning of our project. After all, it was mostly her idea.

The day after our guests arrived, there were practically no sounds from upstairs. Twice a toilet was flushed, but otherwise we heard no voices or the sound of footsteps. No doubt they were exhausted from the trip and the new experiences. Perhaps they slept most of the morning. For lunch, Kathryn cooked a meal of chicken, mashed potatoes and green peas. She said she guessed there were things they might not eat but that everyone eats chicken. When the meal was ready I called up the stairs. Shortly, Mr. Khalif appeared at the top of the stairs. I told him that supper was ready. He responded, "Oh, great. I'll be down in a minute."

Vian disappeared down the second floor hallway. Kathryn and I waited at the bottom of the stairs. Shortly he proceeded down the stairs, alone. At the bottom of the stairs he said, "It smells delicious."

For a moment all three of us stood, looking at one another. I asked Vian if Narin and the children were alright.

"Yes, thank you."

He looked at me, hesitating.

"Oh, did you intend that I should bring them, too?"

I told him, "Yes. Sure."

Kathryn and I glanced at one another again while Mr. Khalif climbed the stairs to collect Narin and the girls. Several days later, Vian whispered to me that it was their normal custom to allow the men of the family to eat first. He said the women eat later with the children. Almost in the way of an apology, he added, "It's an old tradition."

As the days went by, all of us gradually grew accustomed to one another's ways. I learned that Mr. Khalif was the only one who spoke English. The woman and the children spoke only Arabic. During meals, only Mr. Khalif would speak on occasion, but only in my direction and never to Kathryn. The woman and the children never spoke a word at mealtime. Smiling, I noticed, was not part of their normal repertoire.

All went well for a number of weeks. Most days we saw the

Khalifs only at lunch and the evening meal. I made it a point to be present at every meal, doing my errands either before or after meals. Kathryn, who was usually full of talk at lunch and supper, grew increasingly silent at the meals. If words were exchanged it was only between Vian and me. I suspected that Vian had numerous questions about his new environment, but his occasional questions were of the most benign type. His comments could not be interpreted as prying. I, too, tried to avoid questions that might be considered as personal. At lunch one day, trying to make conversation with an innocuous comment, I asked Vian if his family name is a typical Yazidi name. He looked quickly at Narin and, smiling, said that it was not. He then seemed unusually interested in the food on his plate. There was something going on but I was unsure as to what exactly.

Except for lunch and supper, the Khalifs remained upstairs and very quiet. One day, Vian asked me if it would be alright if he, Narin and the girls went for walks in the neighborhood. I told him, "certainly." Subsequently, the four of them went for long walks both after lunch and supper. Invariably Vian and Narin walked side-by-side while the girls followed. On occasion I noticed them out the dining room window. I could tell that Vian usually did most of the talking as I could see him gesturing. Narin never raised her arms but occasionally nodded in apparent agreement to Vian's comments. After several weeks the girls obviously became more relaxed and content with their new environment. At times they would skip along and sometimes grab one another, laughing. Most days the group would be gone on their walks for over an hour.

In time I thought Vian would be interested in finding employment so I inquired on his behalf. Without much effort, I found him a job as a janitor in a local high school. Mr. Khalif expressed endless gratitude. He told me he had been an accountant in Iraq, but he thought he was not as yet ready for that kind of employment in America. I told him I was going to call him Vian because that is our custom in America. I told him he could call me Kevin. As with many things American, he seemed reluctant, but, with some trepidation, went along with his newly acquired custom.

Assuming that Vian would be interested in meeting others of the Yazidi religion, I made some inquiries. A man I contacted, a Yazidi priest, said he would like to come around to meet the couple. I said I am sure Mr. Khalif and his wife would be pleased to meet him. I arranged it as a surprise for the Khalifs. One evening around eight, the priest came to the door. He identified himself as Murad Eesa. I called upstairs to Vian and announced that he had a visitor. As Vian came down the stairs his eyes fixed on the stranger. The gaze never strayed. He seemed tense and uneasy.

"Mr. Khalif this is Priest Eesa."

Vian stopped on the stairs several steps from the bottom.

Behind squinting eyes, he told the man, "How do you do, sir?"

The priest put his hands together much in the Hindu fashion. He said a few words in a foreign language. Vian remained in-place, but said nothing in response. I tried to put the men at ease.

"Gentlemen, shall we go to the living room?"

The two exchanged a few comments in what I guessed was Arabic. I offered to have my wife make some tea but the priest declined. Standing near the front door, he told me, "I think I will be going, Mr. McGroder. I thank you kindly for your invitation."

Strange, I thought. I concluded they were not fond of one another but remained polite. The priest opened the door and let himself out. I decided to let the matter rest and said nothing more to Vian. He went upstairs without a word.

For supper one evening, Kathryn made a mutton shoulder with vegetables and boiled potatoes. A friend of mine had suggested the meal. He told me people from the Middle East especially favor meat from sheep. He was correct. The Khalifs were delighted with the meal. When we had finished eating, Vian placed his napkin on the table and told me, "Mr. McGroder, I have good news. Tomorrow we will be moving out. I thought we would leave after lunch, if that would be agreeable to you?"

Kathryn looked at me, taking in the news. I couldn't read her thought, but I guessed she might have been pleased with the announcement. In a way it seemed time.

I told Vian, "Sure, that would be fine. Will you be alright? I mean financially?"

"Yes, thank you. We shall be fine, again, thanks to your generosity, Mr. McGroder and Mrs. McGroder."

Vian looked first at me and then Kathryn.

I told him, "Whatever you wish. We will be here to see you off."

The next day Kathryn made a lunch of meatloaf and French fries. Meatloaf and French fries were also favorites with the family. For desert, we had more favorites: apple pie and tea. A short time later, Vian, Narin and the two girls came down the stairs. Narin was carrying a small valise. No doubt it contained everything the family owned except for the clothes they wore. Both Narin and the girls were wearing new dresses.

Vian walked over to me and I extended my hand. He shook it enthusiastically. Somehow his handshake suggested a man more confident than the man I had met at the airport three month earlier. A man with improved pride, an improved outlook.

"Mr. McGroder I was fortunate to find a second job, and now I can easily afford rent for an apartment and food. I thank you for your kindness and generosity. I shall forever be in your debt."

I was touched by Vian's words, his sincerity and his gratitude. I was uncertain how to respond. Before I could, Vian continued.

"Mr. McGroder, I must be forthright with you. We are not Yazidis. We are Christians. Narin is my sister and the girls are her daughters. Mr. Baxter, at the American Embassy, knew me from the times when I was an interpreter for the American forces in Iraq. The Islamists had murdered Narin's husband and they were earnestly hunting me. Had it not been for your call, the four of us would most likely have been murdered by now. We hope you understand."

What could I say? Kathryn and I originally hoped to be of assistance to some needy people. Especially children. We had accomplished our goal, although not exactly in the manner we had originally anticipated.

I told him, "Vian, Kathryn and I were delighted to be of help. We wish you, Narin and the girls the best of luck and a secure future."

As Vian moved toward the door, Narin approached Kathryn. When they were near one another, Kathryn placed her hand on Narin's forearm to wish her well. Narin, obviously touched, began crying and said a few words in Arabic. Kathryn was at a loss for words. Vian said that his sister is most grateful for Kathryn's kindness, and she asks that God will watch over and protect her. Kathryn embraced Narin gently. Before the girls walked toward the front door, they curtsied first in front of Kathryn and then me. The door closed and the Kalifs were gone. With a tear in her eye, Kathryn turned to me.

"I'm so glad we had the chance to help them."

I told Kathryn, "Yes. It was a gratifying experience."

We heard nothing more from the Khalifs for several months. Then one afternoon, in a December, Vian stopped by the house. He said he had the day off from work. He brought some cookies his sister had baked for Kathryn and me. Kathryn made tea and the two of us went to the living room where we sipped tea and chatted. He said Narin sends her best regards and best wishes to Kathryn and me. The girls, he mentioned, were attending school and rapidly learning English. "Amazing," he told me, "how quickly the youngsters learn a new language." He reported the four of them were doing well.

When we finished the tea, Vian said he should be going. At the door he commented on the snow that had blanketed the yard that morning. He said the scene was lovely to behold and something he had never expected to see in a lifetime. I asked him to stop by more often, and he said he would. When I offered to drive him home, he begged off. He said he enjoyed walking in the cold air. He said he found it "invigorating." Through the dining room window I watched him disappear down the sidewalk in the direction of the town center.

The Twentieth Reunion
(A fictional short story)

Phil Pritkin spoke into the microphone in an effort to draw attention.

"Testing, testing."

The level of talking hardly lowered as most in attendance remained engrossed in conversations with friends from past years.

"Hello, and welcome to the twentieth reunion of the 1986 class. For those of you who might not recognize me, I am Phil Pritkin. I was in the Law School."

Phil was good speaking on his feet and he was comfortable speaking in front of people. He enjoyed doing it, actually. He often went trolling at socials for clients who had the money to pay for his services. Phil's search for business explained his eagerness to help organize the class reunion. For his joining various social organizations. For his wearing a suit and tie while the other men at the event were dressed "business casual." Phil continued as though everyone was giving him their full attention.

"As you know by now, cocktails are available at the bar. The waiters will start serving dinner at eight. After desert, we will have a few contests. Of course there will be the usual one for the man who has lost the most hair. Another for the woman who has been divorced the greatest number of times. More on the contests and speakers later. The *Devils* band will be playing for your dancing or drinking pleasure. For now, on with the schmoozing. By all means, enjoy yourself. See you around."

Rita Gibson came to the reunion alone and took a seat with acquaintances. Lifting a glass of Pinot Grigio to take a sip, her eyes wandered off to the distance. Two tables over she spotted a woman she thought might be Elaine Winters. *No, that can't be Elaine. But, that sure looks like her.*

"Excuse me, girls, I think I see an old friend. Save my seat. I'll be back in a few minutes."

Taking a roundabout route, Rita came up behind Elaine and put her hands over the woman she recognized as her college roommate.

"Think graduation night, much drinking, sleeping in a van."

"I'm thinking, I'm thinking. Rita Gibson, I'll bet."

"Bingo."

Elaine Winters stood and the two women hugged one another. Elaine stood back at arm's length.

"My Goodness, Rita, you look good. You haven't changed."

"Thank you for the well-intended fabrication. We both know time marches on and it does no favor to anyone in its path."

Elaine told Rita, "Have a seat. We have things to discuss."

"Not right now, thanks. I'm sitting with some girls two tables over. Are you living around Philly or just back for a visit?"

"I moved back with my mother in Hatfield."

Rita told her, "It's noisy here and difficult to hear. Besides, there are too many car and insurance salesmen on the hunt. After supper I'm slipping out. Here's my card. Give me a call. We'll do lunch and get up to speed."

"Oh, it was great seeing you again. I will certainly call."

***

Two weeks after the reunion, Rita went to the Karma Indian Restaurant in downtown Philadelphia where she and

Elaine had agreed to meet for lunch. Upon entering the restaurant, she found it was already half full. Since she didn't see Elaine, she told the waiter she would wait at a table for her friend. She said she would have a cup of tea while waiting. When Elaine entered later she spotted Rita at a table concentrating on her iPhone. As she came near the table, Rita looked up. They embraced again as they had at the reunion and touched cheeks.

Rita told her friend, "It was such a wonderful surprise seeing you again. After all those years. You look really good. It appears you are wearing the same size jeans you had back in school."

Elaine addressed her friend with the nickname she had in college. She told her, "Likewise, Buddy. A delightful restaurant here. Do you come here often?"

"Maybe once a year. There are lots of good restaurants closer to my apartment. You mentioned you like Indian and that's why I suggested this one. It's one of my favorites."

The two smiled, taking a measure of one another. Rita was the next to speak.

"At the reunion, you told me you had moved back with your mother."

"California didn't work out. Kevin and I had problems from the start. The best job he could find was driving a forklift in a warehouse. He did that for the last twenty years and never tried for anything better. One day he didn't come home and didn't bother to call. It turns out he ran off with a bimbo from the warehouse."

"I'm so sorry."

"I went to the warehouse and asked around. I got to talking with one of the forklift operators who had worked with Kevin. He told me that several weeks earlier the super caught Kevin and the floozy screwing on a pile of mattresses."

"What a bum."

Elaine withdrew a tissue from a small compact and touched her eyes. She sighed and took a deep breath before continuing.

"He cleaned out our bank account before he took off. I just walked away from the apartment and left everything there including the dirty dishes. I had to call mother for money to travel back to Philly. You would think the bum would be man enough to call. But he was like that, sneaky and immature. Let the new bimbo learn all that on her own. But, hey, I'm talking too much about me. Sorry. How about you, sweetheart? What's going on in your life?"

"I haven't married. Right after college Mason Hill and I ran around together. For almost three whole years. I'm sure you remember Mason. I kept thinking I would get a ring some holiday, but it didn't happen. He kept pressing me for sex, but, as you know, I come from a very Catholic family. I was a dreamer, and didn't agree to sex before marriage. It's the church's teachings, you know."

"I remember Mason. A real gentleman."

"I loved Mason. I miss him to this day. But, he stopped calling. I heard he moved to Boston where he took a job with a brokerage firm. I gave up going to church. Eleven years ago I bought a beauty shop, and it's been keeping me busy ever since. The shop is only one block away from my apartment. I have five girls working for me, and business has been good. I live alone in an apartment on 22nd Street in the City. Come on, let's try the buffet."

The two women stood and moved toward the buffet with Rita leading the way. They made an attractive duo. Both were of medium height, slender and curvaceous. Rita was a brunette with lustrous hair that had never been colored. She was dressed in a stylish business suit and heels. Elaine was a natural blonde. For their get-together, she dressed in jeans, a shirt and ankle strap sandals. As they passed two middle-aged men seated at a table along the wall, Elaine flashed a smile in their direction. After the women had passed, one of the men looked at his companion and made a thumb up. The second man nodded in agreement.

The two women returned to their table with their selections. After they sat, Elaine took a sip of diet soda and looked at Rita.

"What about boyfriends. Do you have one?"

"No boyfriends. After Mason, I dated a few times, but nothing developed. The way we live today it's hard to meet worthwhile men. I realize my biological clock is ticking, but what's a woman to do?"

Elaine said, "What can I say except that I wish you luck."

Both were silent as they ate while reflecting on memories stirred up. Elaine, pensive, looked at her dear friend again.

"What do you do for entertainment on weekends—or for a vacation? I mean, cooped up here in the City. It seems you don't have a lot of options. Where we lived in San Francisco we could go to the Pacific for water sports or to the mountains for hiking, biking or skiing. We could do both in the same day if we had the desire."

Rita didn't answer. After a pause, Elaine asked, "Do you ski?"

Rita said, "No. Never tried it."

"You should. Skiing is great fun. It gets your mind off your worries. When you are at the top of a slope and looking down, your worries go away. Your only concern is finding the most suitable path down the hillside. It's great therapy. Kevin became an expert skier, and he got me interested."

"Really? Sounds like fun."

"It is. Listen, I made some inquiries since coming back. There's a ski club in King of Prussia. They have a trip going to Colorado in January. I was thinking of going. Why don't we both go to their next meeting? See what's going on?"

"Oh, I don't know. I've never been the athletic type."

"There's nothing athletic about skiing. Maybe just a little. Some people go on the trips just because it's a cheap vacation. It's a great way to meet people. Why don't you come with me to the meeting. We'll have a drink or two. No obligation."

"Ok, why not? Let's plan on it. Let me know the time and I'll pick you up at your mom's house."

***

The chartered 737 jet, carrying 100 members of the King of Prussia Ski Club, landed at the Denver International Airport. The snow-covered Rocky Mountains were visible miles in the distance. Three busses carried the group to Vail, a ski area high in the mountains to the west. Rita and Elaine shared a room at the resort. A ski lift was a convenient, few yards from the hotel. Elaine was the first out of bed the morning after their arrival. She told her friend, "Time to rise and shine. The first ski lessons are at nine."

Rita rolled over and pulled the covers over her head. From under the covers, she responded, "I drank too much wine on the bus. I don't know that I should be doing this. I'm out of my element here. If I break a leg, who's going to watch the shop?

"A broken leg would be a forced vacation. It would be a forced stay away from your business and maybe something you should be doing anyway. You'll be fine. The boots they have these days won't allow you to break a leg. Maybe some other parts, though. Just kidding. Don't be a sissy. Once you are on that hillside and taking in the scenery, you will be thanking me. You'll have fun. Trust me. Ok, Buddy, let's go."

Elaine jerked the covers off Rita and extended a hand to help her out of bed. After she had her standing on her feet, they both proceeded to dress. They went together for breakfast at the hotel's restaurant. Elaine had oatmeal, Rita a bloody Mary. Rita said she needed the drink to settle her stomach and to give her courage for the day to come. Shortly before nine they made their way to the snow-covered hillside near the shack over which a sign read "Ski School." An enthusiastic group had gathered on the packed snow near the shack. Everyone was either in skis or holding a pair in their hands. Most were conversing, exchanging thoughts, comparing equipment, joking. At nine sharp, the door to the shack burst open and three people stepped out and onto the deck. The woman and the two men all wore the same blue-colored parkas that bore the word "Instructor." The woman spoke for the group.

"Good morning, skiers and wannabe skiers. I'm Lisa. My friends here are Marcelo and Michael."

Lisa held a hand in the direction of the man to her right. "This is Marcello. He doesn't know English as well as you, but he knows skiing very well. Marcello smiled and, raising his right arm, waved to the group.

Lisa turned and gestured toward her other companion. "This is Michael. Michael is our all-American instructor from the heartland."

Michael waved to the assembly. Lisa continued.

"In case you haven't noticed, we have beautiful snow conditions today. We're going to have a wonderful time on the mountain."

"Marcello will be taking the advanced skiers, Michael the intermediates and the beginners will go with me. Put on your skis and gather around your instructor."

Rita commented, "Oh, wow. This woman is a fireball of exuberance and enthusiasm. I wonder who winds her spring in the morning."

Elaine turned to Rita.

"You go with the lady. I'm going with Marcelo. This should be fun. See you for lunch at the hotel."

"I don't know about this. I have my doubts. I hope to see you in the hotel and not the hospital."

***

The advanced skiers, including Elaine, gathered around Marcello. Members of the group talked little to one another. They had an air about them that bordered on professionalism. None seemed to feel obligated to speak with others in the group. They all knew skiing at various degrees of an advanced level. After Marcello spoke a few words, the group poled over to the chair lift that would carry them up to a trail marked "expert."

At the top of a trail named "wicked," Marcello stopped to address the group.

"Ladies and gentlemen, down the slope there you will see poles arranged like in slalom race. I go first and through the gates. I then wait below the last pole. Each of you ski through the poles like I did and stop near me. Then we talk again."

The group spent the rest of the morning improving their slalom racing capabilities. Elaine demonstrated she could ski as well as anyone in the group.

Michael spent a few minutes with the intermediates going over the lessons for the day. After he addressed a few questions, his assembly also departed for the ski lift and then to trails of a moderate incline. The morning's lessons concentrated on form and style.

Twenty minutes after Lisa first appeared on the porch at the ski shack, the assembly of beginners was still near the ski shack. Most were full of talk, comparing notes with one another on equipment. One individual forgot her gloves and had to return to her locker in the ski lodge. Another had too much ice on the bottom of his right boot and could not get the binding to close. One after the other, Lisa assisted all of them to solve their respective problems.

Eventually the beginners were ready to proceed with their lessons for the day. Lisa started by leading them to a gentle slope on the other side of the ski shack. At the top of the slope, Lisa told the beginners they were going to practice traversing the slopes. She led the way and, leaning slightly downhill, demonstrated proper form. The first to follow Lisa was a man in a brown parka. He did exactly as Lisa had demonstrated and stopped a few feet short of Lisa. Lisa complimented the man on his performance. Rita was next. Halfway across the slope, her ski tips crossed and she fell. One binding popped open and a ski broke loose. The errant ski slid downhill, gathering speed and then it disappeared into the woods. The man in the brown parka stepped out of his bindings and went in the woods after the errant ski. After he returned, he carried the ski back to Rita. He helped her brush snow from her parka and helped her step into the binding. Standing on both skis, she turned to the man.

"I'm so sorry to cause you all that trouble."

Smiling, the man told her, "No problem. We're all learning as we go."

The remainder of the morning the beginners' group continued practicing their cross-hill skiing. Rita made many more cross-hill traverses, taking extra care to avoid crossing her ski tips.

***

A little after noon, Elaine was sitting with a soda in the hotel restaurant when Rita entered. She asked, "How did it go, snow bunny? Did you enjoy yourself?"

Rita took a seat, and sitting up straight while showing a genuine, fun-loving smile, responded, "Not bad. I actually slid down the hill a few times. At least for short distances. It's more fun than what I had anticipated. But I have a lot to learn. How about you, Miss expert skier?"

"Good. We went to the expert slopes right off. This Marcelo is really a great skier. He's from Argentina. A looker, too."

Rita said, "I watched you go with the expert skiers. You're

pretty good on skis. Are you sure you want to be seen sitting with a snow bunny?"

Elaine merely smiled.

***

Rita and Elaine returned to their ski classes after lunch. Later they returned to their hotel room and slept for two hours. Elaine was the first to rise. She reached over and shook Rita's foot.

"I'm getting hungry. Let's get something to eat. How about some of that western beef and a glass of Burgundy? Maybe the Burgundy first."

Rita turned, yawned and stretched her arms over her head. She told Elaine, "I ache everywhere. I used muscles I didn't know I had."

"Move around. You'll feel better after you limber-up. A glass or two of something will help."

"Ok, ok. I'm hungry, too. And still a little hung over from last night, so, yes, I need some alcohol."

Dressed in their recently-purchased after-ski clothing they went to the Red Lion Inn, a bar next to the hotel. Each had a glass of Burgundy. Elaine was paying the tab when Marcelo entered with a male friend. He immediately spotted Elaine.

"Oh, hi. Elaine, isn't it?"

"Yes, I'm surprised you would remember my name."

"Your's is a name that would be difficult to forget."

Marcello flashed a smile of brilliantly white teeth that contrasted well with his sun-darkened skin and bedroom-brown eyes.

"You know just the right words, Marcelo. Did you learn those lines in Argentina or since you came here?"

"Listen, if you have time—why not you and your friend have a drink with my friend and me?"

Elaine decided to speak for Rita and her. "Sure, we have

time."

The four moved to a table. Marcelo introduced his friend, Felipe, to the women. Felipe was reticent and said nothing. Marcelo explained that his friend spoke very little English and what he knew was limited to a few skiing terms. The conversation was exclusively between Elaine and Marcelo, and the topics were limited to skiing and the adjacent hillside. After a bottle of wine was finished, Elaine said she and her friend had plans.

Elaine told the men, "Thanks for the treat. See you around."

The two women returned to the hotel restaurant where they each ordered a steak. When they returned to their room there was a note under the door.

Elaine, there is a party at High Mountain Hotel, Room 222 at midnight. You and Rita are kindly invited. Hope seeing you there - Marcelo.

Elaine handed the note to Rita. After Rita had read it, Elaine asked, "What do you think?" should we go?

"I'm game if you are. We're not doing anything anyway."

***

A little after midnight Elaine and Rita slipped into their ski parkas. Elaine's was salmon colored, and tight fitting. It was thoughtfully selected back in Philly to display assets. Rita, on the other hand, had a down filled one that was puffy and, according to the salesman at the ski shop, very practical as well as especially warm. They walked to the end of the street and the High Mountain Hotel. Inside, the aroma of burning logs was unmistakable. A gray haired man behind the reception desk didn't bother to look up from the book he was reading. Not seeing an elevator, they climbed the stairs to the second floor. Down the hallway from Room 222 they heard the guitar of Garth Brooks doing "Midnight Sun." The sounds of conversation and laughter from behind the door confirmed a party was underway. Elaine opened the door and quickly raised her hand to her mouth. Inside several dozen naked men and women were lounging about and talking. A few were dancing to the music. She immediately closed the door, and, smiling, turned to Rita.

She asked, "Did you see what I saw?"

Rita said, "Yes. I don't think this is our kind of party."

Elaine stood fast, ready to debate their options, but Rita turned and started to walk away. Elaine joined her friend in walking toward the stairs. As they neared the top of the stairs, the door behind them flew open and Marcello came running out, naked except for a baseball cap. He ran to catch up with Elaine and Rita.

"Girls, please don't go. You are most welcome. There is nothing going on here. It's just a few people pretending to be nudists. No harm. Please."

Elaine looked at Rita and said, "What do you think?"

Rita said, "I'm going back to the hotel. You do whatever you want."

"I don't see any harm. The scene in there reminds me of California. You run along. I'll go in for a few minutes and have a drink. I'll be coming back to the room shortly. I think Marcello will look out for me."

Looking for a confirmation, Elaine looked at Marcelo. Without a word, Rita turned and continued down the stairs. Holding hands, Elaine and Marcello returned to Room 222.

After passing through the front door of the Holliday Inn, Rita went directly to the bar. She ordered a martini, a drink she had tried only once before in her life and years ago. She believed it would be a drink suitable to her need at the moment. She wanted a drink with punch. While squinting from the heat of the vodka she felt a tap on her shoulder.

"Excuse me. Weren't you in the beginners' class this morning?"

Rita turned.

She told the man, "Yes. Oh, I remember you. You helped me with the lost ski this morning."

"Yes. I'm sitting with some other club members over in the corner. Would you like to join us?"

Taking a second glance at the man's profile, she thought the man was not bad looking. He was older than most men on the trip and more her age. He spoke well and looked intelligent. Perhaps her type.

***

At 10:00 o'clock Saturday morning, both Rita and Elaine were still in bed. The preceding night the club had a going-away party at the lower level of the Red Lion Inn. The wine was flowing and all agreed they had a good time. Rita won a gold medal for being the beginner who improved the most. Elaine won honorable mention for having the prettiest woman's tossle cap. Eventually Rita stirred and sat on the edge of her bed.

"Oh, my head hurts. I didn't really need that last glass of wine. We should get ready or we'll miss the bus. I think it's scheduled to be here at noon."

She went to the bathroom. When she returned, Elaine, sitting in a chair by the bed, told her, "I'm not going back to Philadelphia with you. Marcello said I can live with him. In the spring, he'll be returning to Argentina. He said that if I am interested, I can go with him."

"Well, that's a shocker. What will he be doing in Argentina? What will you be doing?"

"Their skiing season starts in March and he has a job waiting for him. I'll learn some Spanish and find some kind of work. Why shouldn't I go? It would be an adventure. There is nothing for me in California or, for that matter, back in Philadelphia. I just need to get away from it all."

"In a way I guess I don't blame you. I hope it works out for you."

"Thanks."

"Well, I have some news for you, too. I'm no longer a forty-two year old virgin. Edwin is a great guy, works for an engineering firm in Philly. He reminds me a lot of Mason."

Elaine threw her arms around her ex-roomie from college days and kissed her on the cheek. Then she told her, "Come on. Let's get dressed. We have time for a little celebration in the bar before the buses arrive. I'm buying."

A little after noon three buses carrying members of the King of Prussia Ski Club pulled away from the Holiday Inn and wound their way through the valley heading in the direction of the Denver airport. The groups aboard were quiet, their vacations at an end. Rita and Edwin sat next to one another near the rear of the second bus. As she took one last look at the snow covered mountains and the majestic spruces, Rita told herself it certainly was a beautiful sight.

Later in the day, Elaine checked out of the Holiday Inn. Carrying Elaine's suitcase, Marcelo walked with her to the High Mountain Hotel. From the hotel's chimney, a column of white smoke spiraled upward into a bright azure sky.

Driving to Work
(A fictional short story)

I anticipated an enjoyable commute to the city. The sky was showing blue to the horizon, and the grass in the fields was once again turning from brown to green. It was a day to be enjoyed after the long, cold winter. I stared my old car and we, the Chevy and I, were ready for the drive to work. I was fond of that car. I had taken loving care of it over the years, and it has served me well. The paint was as shiny as that to be seen in the lot of a new car dealer.

Approaching the interstate highway I accelerated down the ramp and soon was amongst other drivers moving at standard highway speed. That was ten miles an hour above the posted speed limit. It was not a practice I favored, but it was how traffic has been travelling on the roadway for many years. Most drivers feel safe at that speed. Smokey was mostly looking for those who are yet more restless.

I found a tractor-trailer doing standard speed in the right lane and I moved in behind it. With me over in the right lane, drivers of a faster inclination could zoom by in the left or so-called passing lane. My trip was off to a good start. I preferred to stay back a good distance behind the trailer. I called the distance between the trailer and me my safety zone. I had learned that trucks are slower to come to a stop than automobiles. That condition gives me an extra margin of safety. Should the truck driver suddenly hit his brakes, I would have no trouble coming to a stop without banging into the rear of his rig.

All was going well for several miles. The faster drivers were speeding by, eager to arrive at destinations somewhere ahead. My safety zone remained unviolated, and I was enjoying the spring sights. At least that was the situation until an old timer moved up in the left lane and gave a quick tug to his steering wheel, moving his boxy Mercury into my safety zone. How unbecoming! The older folks were usually the slower, more polite drivers, *a la* 1950. Who knows why people behave as they do? Perhaps he had been abused as a youth and was earnest to get back at the world, including all the molesters it harbored. I tried to be understanding. I let up on the accelerator, allowing the Chevy to drop back behind the … gentleman.

After the old guy exerted his democratic right to pull abruptly in front of other drivers, he whipped the big car back into the lane from whence he originated. Accelerating, he moved ahead, no doubt to exercise his right in front of another courteous driver. I relaxed a little, pleased to have my space returned. After all, it was a lovely day. There was no need to become upset over trivialities or rude people. Why accommodate those bent on sowing aggravation?

It was a few more miles before the next offender appeared. That time it was a young miss in a shiny white Beamer. From somewhere to the rear, she zoomed into the recently vacated space in front of me. She had to apply the brakes to avoid crashing into the rear of the trailer. An unseemly behavior for one of the gentler sex. That space must have held some magical attraction to her. In any event, I concluded I preferred to have a pretty young miss as a co-traveler instead of some overweight, cigar-chomping slob. It would be fair to say I did not mind. Perhaps a little! I was inclined to give her the benefit of a doubt considering perhaps she might be new at these highway games. I told myself to be forgiving, charitable. I could do it.

With the young lady travelling in front of me by a few feet, I had to let up on the gas once more to back away. In the past, young women didn't whiz around trying to imitate macho Italian race car drivers. What got into these females of the recent generation? I wondered: Did she zoom in front of only male drivers? Was her commute an opportunity to show distain for bottom pinchers? She was there only momentarily when she returned to the passing lane much as the old guy had a few minutes earlier. I moved up to where I had been, again behind the tractor-trailer and basically unfazed. At least I tried to look at it that way.

For some reason, the tractor-trailer slowed to half of standard speed and briefly swerved off the roadway, spewing gravel and dust into the air. A stone hit the right fender of my Chevy. Damn! I expected to later see a chip of paint missing from that fender. Chances are the driver fell low on coffee or NoDoz. It was time for me to find a tractor-trailer that was staying on the roadway! Looking into the rear view mirror I saw nothing but a steady stream of cars in the passing lane. They were all bunched together with short spaces between one another as they sped by my ear. Nobody wanted to allow anyone into their coveted line. No, that would make their commute milliseconds longer. I had to wait for a chance to break in.

After dozens of cars passed, at last I spotted a car lagging a little. In his red Cadillac the driver was following another vehicle by half the distance recommended by the State Police. The reason for the lag became apparent. The driver was holding a phone and talking enthusiastically to someone far away. With no offense intended, I jerked the wheel to the left and pulled in front of him. One must do what one must do. I needed to get into that line. But the man was unsympathetic. He gave a long blast of his horn and made a display of his hand with one finger noticeably out of place. He moved up to within five feet of my Chevy with the intent of sending a message of some type.

In front of the hothead in the red Cadillac, I found myself going well above standard speed. I had to keep up with the other people in the passing lane. The Chevy's valves were clamoring, begging for relief. At the first chance, I returned to the right lane where I expected to feel more comfortable. The Caddy moved ahead. I stayed on guard in case he would quickly pull in front of me in the way of retaliation. But he proceeded without any additional communications. I was pleased to again be able to enjoy the sights of the farms and cattle, minding my business.

Two muscle cars flew by, one closely following the other. The driver of the rear vehicle was trying to exchange positions with the one in front of him. To be first down the road was no doubt a status of importance to them. But the lead driver was determined to remain in first place. He, too, had his pride. As the pair moved down the road, the two of them swerved from left lane to right lane and back again, the lead driver continuing to block the path of the driver in second place. Chances are that one of them had suffered a bruised ego because of a move made by the other. In that game the lead driver is the winner. I believed that is how they looked at it.

In no time whatsoever, I found another tractor-trailer and moved in behind it. The interstate offered an endless supply of tractor-trailers. Ahead, a cloverleaf came into view and then an on-ramp filled with accelerating cars anxious to move up to turnpike speed or beyond. When I was beside the on-ramp, a juvenile in a Mustang pulled up next to my right side. He was going exactly at my speed. I was undecided. Should I speed up and let him slip in behind me? Or should I slow down to allow him to enter the roadway in front of me? I decided to maintain my speed and allow him to do whatever was his inclination, pull ahead or drop back. He, on the other hand, wanted to play chicken and he moved close to my right fender. I decided I can play chicken too. I had learned that at times courage and bravery are appropriate to the situation. I stepped on the gas a little and he balked. Then he was behind me and, apparently, pissed. What? He expected me to reduce speed so that he could enter the interstate and be in front of me? He decided to take revenge by riding my bumper. Although I had been hoping for something different, the day's commute had become a typical drive to work.

Momentarily, junior became impatient. The right lane was too slow and he could not find an opening in the left lane in the time he had allotted. To show his distain for the interstates' drivers, including me, he went off the road to the right to pass what he considered the slow traffic. Still off the road, he drove past the tractor-trailer before returning to the macadam.

Another few miles and traffic slowed to a crawl. After going many miles at the reduced pace the cause became apparent. Ahead two cars had pulled to the side of the road. Two men were out of the vehicles and exchanging opinions. Automobile parts spread across the roadway told the story. I secretly hoped it was either the old timer in the Cadillac or the juvenile. Maybe the juvenile. Yes, I thought, let it be him. Everyone wanted to have a good look at the car with the buckled hood and the two middle-aged men with waving arms. Once beyond the accident scene everyone increased speed, determined to arrive at their respective destinations without further delay.

A few miles beyond the accident, traffic slowed again. A trooper waiting in a plain wrapper was watching for prey. Enough drivers with radar detectors became aware of the officer and their slowing sent a message to all of their fellow travelers who had no detectors. Once past the trooper, everyone felt the need to make up for lost time caused by the police. I realized I would be late for work. "Shit!" I said out loud.

The slowed traffic seemed to impact peoples' sense of right and wrong. Mostly they felt abused. Drivers began looking for an advantage, for a chance to speed ahead. Courtesy be damned. Along with my fellow travelers, I felt the need to make up for lost time. I moved into the passing lane and nudged the gas pedal downward. I was not the only one. Everyone had the intention to pass someone, anyone, everyone. I was doing alright, starting to make up for lost time. The Chevy did not like it though, but I ignored the sounds of noisy mechanical parts.

In my rearview mirror I saw a shiny, new Jaguar headed my way and moving up quickly. Within what seemed like a few feet, the driver applied the brakes and coasted close to the rear of my Chevy. The message was clear: "Move over misfit." In my rearview mirror I could clearly see the driver was a middle aged woman. True, she had a classy car whereas I had only an old clunker. Was it not expected that an old clunker of a Chevy should make way for an expensive Jaguar? Despite inclinations to remain in the passing lane to show I had pride too, I moved over. She rushed ahead without a "thank you." I was glad to get rid of her. The impolite bitch!

I was almost to my exit and relieved that most of my day's morning commute was almost at an end. I was in the right lane moving along with traffic and looking forward to parking the Chevy in the company's parking lot. Again, someone was on my tail. Low and behold, it was the guy in the red Cadillac. Somehow I had passed him. He was still bearing a grudge from what seemed an event of long ago. I pulled over to the right lane and he moved ahead in the left lane. He no doubt thought he had frightened me to the right lane. But he was wrong. The son of a bitch! It was my turn to provide some angst. I moved to the left lane and hugged the rear of the big Cadillac. We travelled together that way for a spell before I gave it up.

My thoughts of a cloudless day and green fields had vanished. My blood pressure was elevated and my right hand started to twitch. Arriving at my exit, I pulled off the roadway onto the exit ramp. I proceeded to the parking lot near the office where I found a slot, pulled in and turned the ignition off. I took a deep breath. Another day driving to work!

Sirus
(A creative nonfiction short story)

The name is a misnomer: Five Star Hotel. It really isn't a hotel. There are no rooms for rent. All we offer is an old-fashioned bar with cheap beer and cheap whiskey. Our patrons are mostly beer drinkers, people who have little money to throw around but an itch to get out and mingle. They are mostly locals, workers at the nearby race track or, when there are races, people who had wasted their money on the ponies. The stable of the Westmoreland County Race Track is visible in the distance from the parking lot.

I'm only a part-time tender at the bar. My other job is at the stables. One Monday evening a guy by the name of Rick stopped by for a beer. It was a slow night, much as most Monday evenings, and we started talking. He happened to mention the stable boss was looking for a guy to work in the paddocks. The next day I went over to the track and I got the job.

My job is mucking out the horse stalls at the stables. I use a shovel to throw the stuff on a big cart and then haul it to a big dumpster behind the building. Once a week a truck shows up and hauls it away. One day the truck driver told me the stuff is used to grow mushrooms. For some reason mushroom growers use only what comes from the backside of a horse.

First day on the job, I happened to spot Rick trotting a

horse around the track. I stood and watched him for a spell. One of the trainers had told me the Westmoreland races are called harness races. He explained the jockeys ride in a buggy that is pulled behind the horse. The horses are what are called pacers. The other types of races, races with jockeys riding horseback, he said, are called "flats." Those horses, he said, have a different gait altogether.

After Rick put the horse away in its stall he spotted me behind the stable resting on the shovel, thinking.

"Hey, Bart. See you got the job?"

"Hi Rick. Yeah. I should thank you for mentioning the opening here."

"Glad you got the job."

"I think I'll like working here. To tell the truth, I need the money. I'm only part-time at the Five Star and the job doesn't pay much. I'm always running short on cash."

"Just don't let the stable manager find you loafing too many times. That's why he fired the last guy."

I told him, "I'll keep that in mind."

"You say you're short on cash a lot?"

"I don't know where it goes. It just seems to disappear."

"I think we both have the same problem. Look, Bart, you seem to be a decent guy. I'm staying at the Sunshine Motel down the road. It's more money than I would like to pay but it's handy to the stables. Why don't you move in with me and we we'll split the rent? There's only one bed but you could bring in a cot or something."

"Thanks for the offer. Actually, I would like to get out of the place where I'm staying. There are a lot of other things I would rather spend my money on rather than a motel room."

That is how our friendship started. Sunday I moved my things in with Rick. I slept on the floor the first several nights. I had an old quilt I put on the floor and then I would pull a blanket over me. One night I started to put the quilt on the floor. Rick had hung his shirt and trousers in the closet and looked at me with his hands on his hips. Apparently Rick started to feel sorry for me.

"Bart, look, why don't you come and sleep in the bed with me. It's big enough for two. Where I was raised men often sleep in the same bed. No funny stuff. It's only a matter of convenience. A necessity where living space is scarce."

From that day on we started sleeping in the same bed. A bed is definitely better than the floor. Normally there was no problem with our arrangement. Sometimes, though, Rick talked in his sleep. Strange! When he was awake he spoke only English and with no accent whatsoever. He was always, and I mean always, mild mannered. But when he mumbled in his sleep the language was Spanish and often with an angry edge. It was though he was arguing with someone while indignant at the same time.

Rick was a sleep walker. Not often but now and then. One rainy night he got out of bed and shuffled to the front door. It was around two in the morning. I thought he was going to step out in the rain. I asked him where he was going. All he said was, "*mi casa.*" I told him, "Your home is here." He said, "*ah, sí*" and got back in bed. The next morning neither one of us said anything about the episode. I'm sure he didn't remember.

Women sometimes caused complications with our arrangement. Now and then, one of us would have a pickup and would need the motel room for a time. To send a message, we would use a toy jackass, which is also called an ass, that we would put on the windowsill. If one of us came to the motel and saw the jackass, the guy outside was obligated to go elsewhere for a time. Sometimes the jackass was in the window for only a few hours but on occasion it was there until the following morning. We both had other friends, mostly guys from the track, who would let us sleep in their digs for a night. We exchanged the favor when needed. If it was not too cold, there was also the harness room and horse blankets at the stable.

One evening I came to the motel late to find the jackass on the sill. I went elsewhere for the night. At noon the next day the jackass was still there. Again that evening. Some men in my shoes might have been inclined to call Rick and tell him, "Look Rick, either the broad or me." But, no, a real man would not utter those words. Certainly not me. Later Rick told me that the pickup said her boyfriend had kicked her out and she had no place to go. Eventually Rick returned her to a bar, probably the one where he found her. He told me she was not his type. He said the guys at the stable would describe her as one who had been rode hard and put away wet. In typical Rick fashion, he gave her a hundred dollars at the end of the day. For no reason. What the hell, she was only playing the field as best she could. Rick said that before she got out of his car she gave him a big hug and a French kiss. Then she opened the door with one hand and patted him between the legs with the other hand. Rick never wanted to make an enemy. He tried his best to make every parting a pleasant one.

One night I learned "Rick" is not Rick's real name. He is dark skinned and Hispanic-looking. I mentioned to him, "Rick, you sure don't look like a Rick as in Richard."

He smiled.

"You're right. My real name is actually Ricardo Gomez-Mendes. I was born in Juarez. My mother still lives there. God bless her. I like it here and I merely want to fit in. You know, like a caterpillar in a broccoli patch. So I ask people to call me 'Rick.' It sounds more Anglo."

I went bar hopping with Rick several times before I realized my mistake. Although Rick races horses, he is not short and petite like the jockeys who ride the flats. He's also apparently not bad looking. He has that Aztec nose, a regal air, and a killer smile. In the bars you would think the guy had a powerful chick magnet in a pocket. The girls would fawn over him and I would hardly get a glance. It was almost as though I was the invincible man. After placing second a number of times I decided that in the future I would do my bar hoping either alone or with some truly ugly guy. I couldn't get angry with Rick though. Merely because he is good looking is no reason for us not being friends. That would be stupid. Of course we are still good friends. We must be. We live together and sleep in the same bed.

One day at the paddock I was taking a break and eating a cheese sandwich. Rick happened by, walking a beautiful chestnut. When he spotted me, he called over, "Bart, don't take too many breaks or you won't be around long."

I told him, "The boss is away somewhere."

He turned the horse's head in my direction and told me, "Bart this is Sirus."

Looking at Sirus, he said, "Say hi to Bart."

I think Rick gave a tug on the reins at that instant because the horse immediately nodded.

I told the hoses, "I'm pleased to meet you, too, Sirus."

Rick asked me, "Do you mind holding Sirus for a minute while I go get a bucket and sponge. I just walked him after our morning run and I need to cool him down."

"Sure."

I stood up and took the reins with my free hand. The horse did not seem to trust me and kept jerking on the reins. When Rick returned he let the reins fall to the ground. The horse stayed in place, apparently looking forward to a sponge bath.

I asked Rick, "Rick, how many horses do you look after?"

"I'm training two at the present. I don't have time for more than two. Horses take a lot of time and attention."

"Are they your horses?"

"Oh, no. I could never afford these kinds of horses. Besides, a horse is a big expense. Each horse I tend has a different owner. The owners pay me to both take care of their horse and to train them. The stable gets a boarding fee for use of the stalls."

"Sounds like a cushy job."

"No. It's not, believe me. I must feed them, look after their shots, run each one every day for at least an hour. If the owners have doubts about my service, they will quickly find another trainer. My other horse is Damn Fast, a four year gelding."

"Sirus is a beautiful and muscular horse. Who would not want to bet on him?"

Rick gave me a side-glance and told me, "I suggest you stay away from the tracks and keep your money in your pocket. Horse racing is no way to make money."

Several months after I started the job at the stable, Rick stopped by. I was mucking out Damn Fast's stall. Usually we did not talk much at the stable. Rick was always busy with his charges. And, I think, he didn't wish to get me in trouble with the stable boss. Rick was normally a free-wheeling spirit with a ready smile, but that day he was serious. I think he knew my boss was away somewhere. He asked me if I had a minute. I told him, "Sure."

"Maybe we could go out back where we can talk? You know, where we don't have to worry about other ears."

We walked out near the dumpster.

He told me, "You know that chestnut I showed you?"

"Sirus? Sure."

"Sirus is now thirty months old and horsemen call him a two-year old, just the same as if he were a person of thirty months. Next month he will be thirty-one months old and he will then be known as a three-year old—unlike a person. A person would not be considered a three-year old until thirty-six months. Sirus will also start racing with other three-year olds as well as older horses."

"Ok."

"I can tell you Sirus is a winner. What I mean to say is that I have been holding him back in the dozen or more races that we have been in. Very few people in the stands can tell that I was keeping him from going up front. They can see the reins but there is no way of knowing whether I am pulling back or throwing them to the pony. We have been finishing mainly in the middle of the pack."

"You planned it that way?"

"Yes, I was purposely holding him back. Anyway, Sirus is a strong horse and he wants to run faster. Next Friday the owner has Sirus booked in a race in Jersey. It's a popular track and there will be lots of money in the bets. I'm going to let Sirus run with the wind. Chances are he will win the race. No guarantee, but chances are good. Better than good."

"Wow. Good luck."

"There is more. You and I are going to make some money Friday. That is, if you're game."

"What do you mean 'game'? What do I have to do? I don't want to go to jail over a few dollars."

"No, nothing like that. Here is what I propose. You take the day off and drive to the track alone. You don't talk to me here at the stables or in Jersey. You act like a normal man out for the afternoon to bet on horses. Sirus is running in the fifth race. He'll be horse number four. Because of the horse's modest performance in past races the odds on him will be fairly high. You are going to bet a hundred and fifty dollars for yourself and the same for me. More than that would drive the odds down and might also raise suspicions. You don't place all of the bets at one window. No, you make small bets at different windows. You wait five or ten minutes between the bets. At every race there are a few guys who bet on the long shots, so it will look normal. Are you in?"

"What if we get caught?"

"We are not doing anything illegal. We are merely betting on a horse. Believe me this happens all the time. Guys in the stables will know what is going on, but nobody is about to speak up. They all do it when they can. Here, I wrote it down for you. Horse number four in the fifth race. Take the piece of paper with you so you don't forget."

Rick handed me the piece of paper.

"Ok, I'm game."

"I'll give you my money next week."

The following week Rick and I went to the Jersey track as planned. He went with the horse trailer. I drove my old Chevy. In the fifth race Sirus was slow out of the gate. Half way around Rick was boxed-in and had no place to go. I figured I not only wasted the day but a hundred and fifty bucks as well. I started thinking how many beers that money would have bought. Why did I trust Rick on this? But coming down the home stretch the horse to Rick's right broke gait and fell back. Rick did a quick right and came out of the box. Sirus won by half a length. Rick and I split the winnings of seven-thousand dollars.

Sirus's owner had bet only twenty dollars on the horse to win. Nevertheless, I think he was delighted at Sirus's performance. If he suspected Rick of anything, he never said a word to Rick. Chances are he didn't care one way or the other.

He had learned he had a winner and that was every horse owner's dream come true.

We went back to our stables after the race in Jersey. I saw Rick get a thumbs up from another trainer, but I suspected nobody said a word. No doubt the other trainers had their secret hopes for their day with a promising two-year old.

A few days after the race I saw a money order of three-thousand dollars on the chest of drawers where Rick kept his things. It was near an envelope addressed to Seniora Isabella Gomez-Mendez, Jaurez, Mexico. I realized then why Rick spent very little money on women or himself. Why he drove on old beat-up Chevy with peeling paint and cracked seats.

Encounter on Line Mountain
(A creative nonfiction short story)

It was an hour before sunrise when I parked my SUV near the base of Line Mountain. After I took hold of my shotgun and the necessary flashlight, I headed through the laurels and in the direction of a particular hillcrest. That day I would be hunting alone. When I went for deer, rabbits or pheasants I usually went with hunting buddies, but in the spring gobbler season my preference was to go solo. My wife didn't favor my hunting alone, but a single hunter has a better chance of harvesting a gobbler. And going for gobblers in the spring was my favorite hunting sport. So, it was a risk I willingly took.

In the spring, the birds are in the mating mode. The challenge to the hunter, and the proper way to hunt a gobbler, is to imitate the call of a hen turkey looking to mate. Doing the call well is a challenge and an accomplishment. If the call is true, a gobbler may answer and possibly will approach the source of the calling. Gobblers can be warry and, for a bird with a brain the size of a walnut, they can be surprisingly smart and wary. If the hunter can coax the gobbler within shotgun range, the hunter may have a chance for success. No guarantees, though! If the bird spots motion, the slightest motion, it will vacate the area in a flash.

From previous scouting trips, I learned at least one gobbler favored an area at the crest of a ridge a few miles from where I parked the car. While in the valley, I had heard gobblers calling up on top of the adjacent ridge to the south. I had decided then that those gobblers would be the object of my hunt in the near future. My plan for the hunt was to be at the top of that ridge well before sunup. I expected the climb up that mountainside would take over an hour. It was a high mountain with a steep hillside, but I didn't consider that an obstacle. I was in good condition from running. To tell the truth, I figured the heights would eliminate some of the competition who might find the climb too arduous.

Flashlight in hand, I continued along a trail that wound half way up the hill. The rest of the climb would be through laurels and over deadfalls. It was warm and after 30 minutes of climbing, I stopped for a rest. My camouflaged shirt was becoming moist. Shortly after I left the trail, a turkey flushed from a nearby tree. I heard the beat of its large wings, but in the dim light couldn't see it as it made its way through the treetops. A little farther, a deer snorted and the scampering of hooves in the dry leaves followed the announcement.

When I arrived at the summit of the mountain, dawn was beginning to break. I found a seat at the base of a large oak and rested while I waited for the forest to come alive around me. I had always found the early part of May to be a wonderful time to be the Pennsylvania woods. The songbirds were awakening and beginning to call one another. In the distance a great horned owl gave one last call before, no doubt, retiring within the foliage of a tall hemlock. As quietly as possible, I loaded three shells into my shotgun as I prepared for the action I hoped would follow. Soon it would be time to call.

Sometimes I used a barred owl call to locate a gobbler. It's a call that is easy to imitate and sometimes helps to locate a gobbler. At first light, a gobbler is inclined to be vocal and will often sound off with loud gobbles in response to other sounds of the woods. Gobbles are inclined to announce their presence and availability to hens in the vicinity. Whereas the owl call will often cause the gobbler to respond, I learned other birds might likewise show interest. Barred owls often fly over to the sound either to meet a mate or to start a fight. Crows will sometimes come looking for a rumble with the owl. If I locate a gobbler, I will generally approach within 200 yards and then use a slate call to imitate the calls of a supposedly interested hen.

Aside from the response from gobblers, a hen call can elicit a variety of responses. On occasion, I've had wolves come to the calls. (Some people call these canines in the wilds of Pennsylvania "coyotes." I call them "wolves" because the DNA of these canines are more wolf than any other mix.) Naïve hunters will sometimes try to sneak up on the source of a hen call, and that is always a concern.

After enjoying the scene and the sounds at the top of the mountain, I was ready to begin the hunt. Because I expected a gobbler was nearby, I decided to start right off with a hen call. With my slate call I gave a few soft mating calls. I thought they came off well. Essentially, I was saying to the gobbler, "Here I am, and I'm looking to party. Where are you?"

Within seconds of my first call, I heard rocks sliding below the crest of the mountaintop to the north of my position. I found the sounds puzzling. Turkeys are much too agile to cause rocks to slide. Likewise, sure-footed deer could not be the cause of rocks sliding. Because of their slender legs, deer avoid rocks and the potential for a broken bone. Looking in the direction of the sound, I was startled to see a bear cub come running up to the plateau. The cub apparently heard the turkey call and, curious, intended to investigate. It was running exactly toward my position.

At first I found the sight of the young bear thrilling. Despite my many days in the woods, I had never seen a bear. I had seen bear sign but never one in the flesh. As the cub continued in my direction, I shortly became concerned that it might bump into me. Or, startled, it might take a swing at me. It was a second year cub and relatively large for a cub. Black bears in Pennsylvania are known to be the largest in the world. Here they find an ample supply of food in both nearby farms and the large wooded tracts. Some will grow to the 600 and 700 pound range.

To avoid a collision with the cub, I waved my arms. It saw the motion and, then, me. Startled, it ran to the nearest tree, a large red oak, and placed his forelegs around the tree. It climbed up the tree a few feet and then gave up the climbing inclination. It returned to the base of the tree and merely sat there, looking around. While focused on the cub sitting a mere 20 feet away, I detect motion in the corner of my eye. It was another bear—a large bear!

The second bear was no doubt the mother of the cub. It was at a distance of 100 feet and standing on its rear feet with the front paws withdrawn, unmoving. It was watching the area around the cub in an effort to determine what was going on. The sow seemed suspicious while remaining in the same position. I enjoyed the scene. The large bear did not see me for the reason that I was in full camouflage and still. In due time, I decided I must return to turkey hunting and I should allow the bears to go about their business. I stood up and removed the camo face mask. I expected both bears to scram—as bears are expected to do when they see a human. However, both bears were nonplused by my presence. I waved my arms to be certain the two saw me, but both bears showed no response.

The sow dropped to all fours and began to walk toward the cub and me. The cub remained sitting, indifferent to it all. I became flummoxed by the situation developing in front of me. When the large bear came to within 50 feet, I decided it was time to put distance between the bears and me. Besides, I told myself, I climbed that mountain to hunt a gobbler and not for the purpose of watching bears. It was time to get on with it. I stood and started walking east along the crest of the mountain and, I hoped, away from the bears. I expected there would be a gobbler somewhere out there.

Glancing over my shoulder I noticed the mother bear came to the base of the tree where I had been sitting. I guessed the size to be in the 400 pound range, a powerful beast. Head to the ground, it picked up my scent and continuing to walk in the path I had taken. In fact, it was gaining on me. The cub was following behind its mother. I started walking faster but the bears did likewise. When the sow was at 20 feet I was forced to stop and face it. I could not allow the bear a chance to rush my back. Its head was low to the ground and its ears were held down. It looked fierce and angry—ready to charge. I became concerned. The sow's small black eyes were focused on me and only me. For some reason the bear continued to consider me a threat to the cub. Or, perhaps, it was angry to find me near the cub. Who knows what bears think?

Although large and generally slow moving, bears can move with lightning speed whenever they choose. It could be on me in seconds. Whereas I had in my hands a shotgun loaded with three shells, I doubted the potential of the weapon to stop a large, charging bear. Bears are very difficult to kill, and a shotgun loaded with bird shot might not be enough to stop a charge. I did not wish to needlessly kill the bear. Besides, I thought shots from a shotgun might only make the bear more angry and vicious.

When the bear was ten feet away and still walking toward me, I fired once in the ground near its front paws. I hoped the sound would discourage the bear from continuing its forward march. I had decided the next two rounds, if needed, would be for the bear. Sticks and dirt flew up from where the shot hit the ground. The sow seemed to take the shot as a warning. It stopped but did not retreat. Gradually I backed away, keeping my gun at the ready and aimed at the animal. It remained in-place as I continued to widen the distance between us. Once it turned to check on the cub, but its gaze returned to follow me.

At a distance of 100 feet I came to a trail that went along the crest of the ridge. After one last glance to be certain the bears were not in pursuit, I turned and ran out along the trail. As I moved along the trail, I kept looking for trees with branches low enough that would allow me to climb up a tree. I had never considered climbing a tree in the woods, so this was a new search. There were no suitable trees. I was in an old forest and all the branches that could be used for climbing were much too high above ground level. Out of breath, I slowed my pace to a walk. Turning, I confirmed the bears were no longer following me.

Eventually I spotted a deer hunter's treestand that had associated steps nailed to the tree trunk. The treestand had been built many years in the past and the wood of both the steps and the treestand appeared to be deteriorated. Nevertheless, I thought it might be adequate for my purposes. I thought that if needed, I might be able to climb up into the treestand. I had a strap on my shotgun, and that would allow me to climb while taking the gun with me. I stopped and watched for the bears. If they came at me again, I would be climbing up into the treestand. Watching in the direction of the bears, I saw them as they moved slowly but somewhat in my direction. Fortunately, it seemed they lost interest in me. Together, they moved down from the crest of the hill, out to the west and well below my elevation. After they had disappeared from sight I heard their movements in the dry leaves for a time. I remained near the treestand long after the sounds of their movements.

After waiting for a period, I decided I should resume the hunt for a gobbler that I knew was somewhere nearby. I attempted to reorganize my thoughts and to plan a strategy for the remainder of the morning. It occurred to me that I should load another shell in my shotgun to replace the one I used to stop the bear's advance. Taking a shell from my pocket I realized for the first time that my hand was shaking. It was the first time I ever remembered having a shaking hand. The bears had me rattled.

Strange! As I stood near the treestand, my thoughts returned to a day in the French Alps when, a few years in the past, I had experienced another near-death occurrence. It was in October of the year and I had hoped to drive through a mountain pass from France into Italy. To my surprise there was snow at the high elevations. The depth increased the farther I drove. Eventually it was too deep for further travel, and I was obliged to turn around. The road was much too narrow to allow a turn-around in the road, so I backed my Volkswagen into a small space to the side of the road. However, the car skidded when I tried to return to the road. I tried several times with no luck. The car had moved sideways from skidding on the snow. When I looked out the side window I could see straight down for hundreds of feet. There were no guard rails. One more foot and the rear wheel would go over the edge. I thought I would have one more try and that would be it. With luck the tires caught traction and I pulled back onto the road. Only after I had descended from the heights of the Alps, did I fully appreciate the severity of my near-death experience. My hand was not shaking at the time, but I stopped in the first bar and ordered a double Cognac.

Gathering my thoughts, I walked quietly in a westerly direction and beyond the spot where the sow caused a ruckus. Finding a likely location again further out of the crest of the ridge I rested for a few minutes. I prepared to resume calling, but gradually I recognized how unnerved I had become. I concluded that under that state of mind I could not enjoy any additional hunting that day. It was time to go home. Reluctantly I grabbed my gun and started the trek down the mountainside. I would return another day!

I was pleased that I had avoided shooting at the large bear. The consequences might have been fatal to both the bear and me. I later learned that some families in the nearby valleys were feeding bears. That practice probably explained why the animals of my encounter had lost their innate fear of humans.

I gave up turkey hunting the year the bears chased me on Line Mountain. The following year, though, I was at it again. One afternoon, and later in the season, I was hunting near the spot where the sow came after me. It was after shooting hours, and I would soon be returning home. I approached the tree where I was sitting when the cub came running up from below the rim of the mountain. For no reason whatsoever, I took the seat I had when the cub first appeared. I recalled the events of the encounter, placing them in the proper sequence. The sun was at high noon and the black flies were stirring. In an adjacent pine tree an assembly of blue jays seemed to be arguing about a topic of importance to them.

Comes Around
(A creative nonfiction short story)

Lieutenant Mason Baxter was not looking forward to visiting the enlisted men's club. The news was rarely good. He inserted his key into the rear door of the building and entered. Inside, Corporal Jennings was rearranging the chairs. When he heard Baxter enter, he turned and greeted the lieutenant.

"Not a bad night, lieutenant. No fights, no missing utensils or broken chairs. The take wasn't bad either, around two-sixty."

Of course, the mentioned "take" did not include the twenty dollars that Jennings had earlier slipped into his pocket. According to a prior agreement with the lieutenant, Jennings was entitled to ten percent of gross. But he had another agreement with himself, and that was to skim an extra twenty every night for his personal cause. He would have liked to treat himself to more, but he figured that might invite suspicion.

The lieutenant told him, "If only we could repeat that every evening."

The enlisted men's club at the US Army's Hilgen Depot, Germany, was similar to many US Army enlisted men's clubs worldwide. It was a place where the post's soldiers could find cheap beer, entertainment and kindred spirits. Every army base of any size has an enlisted men's club. Army brass consider the enlisted men's clubs as necessary establishments that help keep the post's soldiers on base and out of trouble with the locals. The higher-ups considered it best to keep drunk soldiers on base rather than have them staggering down Hochstrasse looking for mischief to be done. The presence of the clubs mean less headaches for all concerned. Besides, most enlisted men at army posts have limited means of transportation and little cash to consider alternatives other than what was to be found on post.

As he had done every evening for the last five months, Lieutenant Baxter counted the cash. Turning to Jennings, he handed him thirty dollars and told him, "Here's your share. The rest goes to the safe. See you tomorrow, same time."

"See you, lieutenant."

Most enlisted men at the post showed deference to officers as required by army protocol. It's the only way an army can function. However, Baxter and Jennings had a common need that trumped protocol. Both needed one another and for this reason they tended to treat one another as equals. Neither could afford to aggravate the other. Baxter turned and headed for his Volkswagen. He was both hungry and thirsty.

***

In town, Baxter parked near the Stilts Gasthouse, his favorite local source for German meals, and, what is more important, German beer. Entering, he spotted another lieutenant from the post, Lieutenant Bart Carver. Carver was eating alone. Both were platoon leaders in the 678th Ordnance Company, and they had much in common. Carver waved him over to his table and motioned to the chair opposite him. A waitress appeared in a matter of seconds.

"Good evening, lieutenant. Would you like the usual?"

"Yes, a draft, please."

"Light or dark? We have dark starting this week."

"I'll stay with light."

"Yes, sir."

Carver asked, "How's it going, Mason? Still having fun at the enlisted men's club?"

"Funny! Very funny! Maybe a beer or two will help me forget the damn thing."

"How much you out this month?"

"Somewhere over a hundred so far. But there are still ten days to go in this month. So, it could be closer to one-fifty before the month is over."

"All the officers at the post know your dilemma. I suspect they all feel sorry for you, particularly the ones who had the club in the past. Yet, nobody I know would like to take it off your hands."

"That is very consoling. Thank you for the thought for the day."

"Tell me something, Mason. Why is the colonel making you keep the club for so long. What is it now? About seven months? Does he have it in for you for some reason?"

"Eight, going on nine. I don't know his thinking. It's impossible to understand him or what makes him tick."

"Wow. That is strange. I was told that normal practice in the past was to change managers every three months. That way the pain is spread around. Who can afford to have it for much more than a month or two let alone seven?"

"Tell it to Colonel Forney."

Baxter's beer arrived, and the waitress asked, "Would you like something to eat, sir?"

"Yes, I'll have the schnitzel with dumplings and red cabbage."

"Very good. Your favorite if I remember correctly."

After the waitress had taken a few steps to draw the beer, Carver said, "That Colonel Forney—one of my clerks said he knew of him back at Fort Belvoir. The two were there at the same time. He said the colonel is strictly a pencil pusher, a desk jockey with no troop experience. He got promoted by following the old rule: do nothing, make no decisions and thereby avoid trouble. According to the reports, nobody liked him there either. The man's out of his element as commander of troops. He never talks with anyone, enlisted men or officers, so there's no spreading of the information there. Mason, you have my sympathy. Hey, the beers are on me tonight. Cheer up."

***

The next time Mason visited the Enlisted Men's Club, the news, was disappointing. Corporal Jennings reported, "Lieutenant, we had another fight last night. They broke a table and smashed two chairs. It seems that while all of that was happening somebody made off with utensils for four settings. I was too busy trying to stop the fight, so I couldn't see what was going on behind my back. You know some of these guys wait for a distraction before slipping these things into their pockets. Probably some married guy who lives off post. I didn't recognize any of the guys in the fight. I think they were visiting from another post. I called the MPs but all the troublemakers disappeared before they showed."

Mason thought to himself. *Strange. Jennings never seems to see anything.*

Of course, Mason realized that Jennings would have a problem if some of his fellow enlisted men considered him a snitch. Besides, he no doubt figures that Mason and the other officers can afford to lose a little since they receive many times the pay of enlisted men. Better to never see anything.

"What's the bill come to this time?"

"Looks like about $85."

"Fine! Just fine! If this keeps up, come payday I'll be owing the government money."

The army's rules for operation of the enlisted men's clubs are strange. The government provides the building, everything in the club and the cost of the utilities. However, every club has an officer in charge of the club's operations. And, that officer is pecuniarily responsible for everything in the club. If, for example, a table disappears the officer in charge of the Enlisted Men's Club pays for it out of his pocket. Actually, the funds are taken from his paycheck so, actually, it is money he never sees. That is the army's way. Because the Enlisted Men's Club is a lose-lose proposition, no officer willingly takes responsible for the club.

Baxter said, "I am going to see Colonel Forney again. This isn't right. I cannot take this much longer. If I cannot get some relief I am resigning from the army. To hell with this business."

Mason did not actually intend to resign his commission if things didn't go his way. His words were merely an outward expression of disappointment and disenchantment. Enlisted men cannot suddenly determine that they do not care to be in the US Army any longer, but actually officers have other options. If an officer no longer wishes to be an officer, the army no longer wishes to have him in a position of responsibility. He's out and promptly.

***

Lieutenant Baxter was near the end of his patience and decided a visit to Colonel Forney was in order. When he stepped up to the colonel's clerk in the headquarters building, the clerk asked, "May I help you lieutenant?"

"Yes, I would like to have an appointment with the colonel at his convenience."

"Let me check the colonel's schedule."

Withdrawing Colonel Forney's appointment book, the clerk suggested, "How about tomorrow at 1 p.m.? May I tell the colonel the purpose of your appointment?"

"It's about the Enlisted Men's Club."

"Fine, sir. I'll tell the colonel. We'll see you tomorrow at 1 p.m."

***

At the designated time, Mason reported to Colonel Forney. According to army protocol, Mason saluted and remained at attention in front of the colonel's desk, pending acknowledgement by the colonel. Unlike most senior officers at the post, Colonel Forney's practice was to delay telling a young officer to be at ease. It seemed to be his way of letting them know he was the boss and in charge. In due time he told Mason to be at ease, but he did not invite him to have a seat at the chair that was two feet to the left of Mason.

"What's on your mind lieutenant?"

"It's the Enlisted Men's Club, sir."

"Oh, that again? What's the problem now? We discussed this matter months ago."

"Yes, sir; we did. It was two months ago. Sir, I would like to remind the Colonel that I have been in charge of the Enlisted Men's Club now for almost seven months. I have been glad to do my part as, I'm sure, have all of the other officers who had the club in the past. However, it has been very expensive for me. So far I have found it necessary to pay over nine-hundred dollars for damaged and stolen property. It's a very difficult situation, sir, as I cannot be at the club every minute it is open. As you know I have my regular Company duties during the day. I respectfully suggest that perhaps it is time for another officer to take over management of the club. I've been told that in the past it has been practice to change officers every three months."

"Baxter, if you were a better officer you would run a better show. You would be making the enlisted men pay for things they break or steal. Frankly, I have not been impressed with your leadership capabilities. I don't think you will be ready for promotion to first lieutenant when the time comes around. That's all Lieutenant."

"Yes, sir. Thank you sir."

Mason stood smartly, saluted, turned and exited the room. Once on the street he whispers to himself, *One son of a bitch.*

Lieutenant Baxter's dilemma went on for another month. During that period, he became resentful of his dilemma, but he did not wish to be considered a quitter. He decided to stick with the club and somehow work through the problem. In time, though, the many hours he was spending at the post began taking a toll on both his health and his mental state. He started losing weight and dark circles appeared around his eyes. His sense of humor disappeared. He found little time for friends, reading or relaxation of any type. He started drinking more German beer to blur thoughts of what appeared to be a problem with no solution in sight.

All seemed bleak to Mason and he could not see any relief in the foreseeable future. Then, a light suddenly appeared in the darkness. One evening at the club, Jennings, who was aware of the strained relationship between Colonel Forney and Lieutenant Baxter, related some unanticipated news. He told the lieutenant, "Lieutenant, I was wondering if you heard about Colonel Forney?"

"No, I haven't seen him or heard anything about him for at least a month."

"Did you hear he was passed over on his second review. I heard that from a friend of mine who has it from a reliable source. No names mentioned."

There is an army rule that applies to officers without exception. Every officer is periodically reviewed for promotion. The necessary time in grade is proscribed by army rules. If an officer is not promoted in two consecutive reviews, he is automatically relieved of duty. In other words, he is ousted from the army. That is common knowledge to anyone serving in the army. Mason's spirits lifted.

Mason replied, "Really? No, I didn't hear that."

Jennings said, "There is more to the story. My friend said the colonel is only five months from retirement eligibility, and he is considering reenlisting as a non-commissioned officer."

If a soldier leaves the army after twenty years of service, that soldier is entitled to a pension along with a pay raise every year until death. For an officer of the rank of colonel, the monthly paycheck would be a tidy sum. For those short of the eligibility date–nothing. However, the army has an option for ex-officers. They are eligible to sign up as an enlisted man, and the combined time in the service counts toward retirement. And, the retirement pay is based on the highest pay rate during the twenty years of service. Upon re-enlisting, an ex-officer would automatically be given the rank of sergeant. Reenlistment was the option Colonel Forney chose. That gave him the opportunity to collect his pension if he would only serve as a sergeant for a short period. What Forney didn't anticipate was that he would be assigned to Lieutenant Baxter in operating the enlisted men's club. It seemed the post commander was aware of the problems at the club and the unfair treatment that the colonel had visited on the unfortunate lieutenant. Besides, he thought Colonel Forney unsuited to be a US Army officer let alone a colonel.

The first day on the new assignment, Sergeant Forney reported to Lieutenant Baxter at the club. The lieutenant had been informed that Sergeant Forney would be reporting for duty and he was ready for him. The sergeant walked up to the lieutenant, without saluting, and started to speak.

"Lieutenant, perhaps you heard..."

Lieutenant Baxter interrupted him:

"Sergeant, did I ask for your opinion?"

Sergeant Forney could not afford to be found disrespectful to an officer. A lucrative pension was at stake. Of all things, he did not wish to be dishonorably discharged short of the magical twenty years.

Sergeant Forney replied, "No, sir."

Lieutenant Baxter told him, "Hereafter, I will expect you to submit an opinion only when one is requested of you. Is that understood?"

"Yes, sir."

The lieutenant told him, "Sergeant, exit the building the way you entered. I suggest you take ten minutes to give serious thought to your situation here. Report back to me in exactly ten minutes. The next time you report I expect you to follow army rules. You will salute and stand at attention until directed to do otherwise. Is that understood?"

"Yes, sir."

"Now go."

As ordered, Sergeant Forney exited the building and in ten minutes returned to report to Lieutenant Baxter. He approached Lieutenant Baxter and saluted.

"Sir, Sergeant Forney reporting for duty as ordered."

Mason saluted smartly but did not tell Forney to be at ease. Slowly, Mason walked around the sergeant with the three new stripes on his sleeve, examining his clothing. After a time, he told him, "At ease, Forney. I see your shoes need a shine, your trousers are lacking a crease and your brass is dull. Your uniform is in disgusting condition. When you report tomorrow I will expect you to be in better condition. Now, report to Corporal Jennings. He will give you your work assignments for this evening."

Thus began the remainder of Sergeant Forney's stint at the Hilgen Depot Enlisted Men's Club. For a time, it became pure hell for the once-inconsiderate, ex-colonel, Sergeant Forney. Every time he reported to the Enlisted Men's Club for duty, Lieutenant Baxter made it a point to inspect him. The lieutenant would always find something amiss with the sergeant's uniform. The lieutenant tried to make sure there would be a number of observers nearby so as to magnify the embarrassment effect. But, the lieutenant's opportunities for continuing revenge came to an end exactly one week after Sergeant Forney had first reported for duty at the club. It started with a call from the clerk to the new Commander of Troops, Colonel Robert Watkins. He told Lieutenant Baxter. "Sir, Colonel Watkins would like to see you at your earliest convenience."

In army speak, the message translated to, "Drop whatever you are doing and come here quickly."

Lieutenant Baxter replied, "I will be there promptly."

Upon entering Colonel Watkin's office, Lieutenant Baxter saluted smartly.

"Lieutenant Baxter reporting, sir."

Unlike the colonel's predecessor, Mason was promptly told, "At ease, Lieutenant. I am not going to ask you to have a seat. What I have to say will take only a minute. It is my understanding that you have had responsibility for the Enlisted Men's Club for an extended period. I do not know how that happened. I mean for a long period like that. Anyway, it is time for another junior officer to take over. I am assigning Lieutenant Jason Schmidt to be responsible for the club effective tomorrow. So, you two get together and arrange for transfer of the government property. Unless you have something to discuss, that is all I have for you."

"No, sir, I have no other issues of importance. Thank you, sir."

Mason snapped to attention, saluted sharply, turned and stepped smartly to the door.

Once away from the building, Mason was inclination to shout with joy, but he knew that would be un-officer like. He managed to restrain his emotions while keeping a poker-face.

Lieutenant Schmidt, the new officer responsible for the Enlisted Men's Club, reported to the club at the appointed time, and Lieutenant Baxter showed him around. They went over the books as well as the cash in the safe. All of the government's property was present according to the manifest except for ten dinner knives. Baxter had to pay for those, but he had no objections since that would be the last of his payments. Before departing the Enlisted Men's Club for the last time, Lieutenant Baxter walked over to Corporal Jennings and briefly spoke with him. They shook hand and then Baxter disappeared through the back door.

Eventually, Sergeant Forney's completed his twenty years of active duty and his assignment at the enlisted Men's Club came to an end. He departed for the States to start his retirement and his government pension.

On Mason Baxter last day at the club, he bumped into Lieutenant Bart Carver at Company Headquarters. In an exceptionally cheerful mood, he said, "Hey Bart, if you are not doing anything tonight I'm buying the beers at the Stilts Gasthouse."

"Free beers. I'll be there. What's the event?"

"All I'll tell you is that it's a comes around celebration."

"Whatever. See you tonight."

Hamburgers
(A creative nonfiction short story)

Eric was the first to stir in bed. The wine he was imbibing the night before left him with a dry tongue and a stomach in revolt. He was not really looking forward to another day of viewing cathedrals and such where few people spoke his language. His moving about awakened his wife, causing her to turn over and then, putting her feet on the floor, go for the bathroom.

Eric and Melissa Kramer were from Butler, Pennsylvania. They both worked at full-time jobs and had managed to save some money over the years. In fact, they managed to save more than a little. Eric owned and ran three beer distributorships that he inherited from his parents. Business had been good. Melissa, to get out of the house, was a nurse at a high school.

At cocktails one evening, months earlier, it was duly noted that their twentieth wedding anniversary was approaching. It was agreed that perhaps a special vacation was in order. Maybe a trip to somewhere out of the country. Neither one had been out of the country. Their two daughters were off to college and fully occupied. So they would not be a hindrance. After a visit to a nearby travel agency, the couple decided on a trip to Paris.

Returning from the bathroom Melissa planted a gentle kiss on Eric's cheek. Melissa was enjoying the sights and food of Paris.

"Time to rise, sweetheart. We're scheduled to meet the bus at ten o'clock. If you want breakfast, you better get moving. Up and at 'em, cowboy."

Melissa sat on the edge of the bed next to her husband in an effort to arouse interest in the day's schedule.

"Breakfast is part of the package. If you don't want anything to eat, I'll go down myself."

Eric mumbled, "You go ahead. I'm not hungry."

Hotel Opal had a small room off the lobby where simple breakfasts were made available for guests. Other members of the tour were already having coffee and pieces of baguette. Melissa took a seat in the small room. A couple was seated at the next table. The man had a full head of red hair with touches of white at the temples. She was attractive. Both were nattily dressed. They appeared to be professionals of some type and refined.

A waitress appeared at Melissa's table.

"Café, madam?"

"Yes, please."

"Would you like a croissant au beurre or perhaps some bread and jam?"

"How about toast?"

"No, sorry. I vill bring you fresh baguette and jam. Baguette is like toast. You will like it I sink."

The couple at the adjacent table spoke to one another briefly and then the woman turned to Melissa.

"It appears you are eating alone. Why don't you join us."

"Oh, thank you. I will. I don't believe my husband will be having anything to eat this morning."

Melissa rose and took one of the two empty chairs at the couple's table.

The man spoke first.

"My name is Macarten Meegan and this is my wife Rosheen."

"I'm Melissa Kramer."

Rosheen, her green eyes a perfect match to the scarf she wore around her neck, looked at Melissa.

"From your accent, I would guess you are from the States. Am I mistaken?"

"No. I mean yes. I am from Butler actually. That's a small town in Pennsylvania."

The waitress approached with coffee and sliced pieces of baguette, all of which she deftly placed in front of Melissa.

"Will that be all, madam?"

"Yes, thank you."

"And your room number if you please?"

"322"

"Sank you."

After the waitress was well away from the table Melissa commented, "The people are so courteous here."

Mark smiled.

"You will never get anywhere with a Frenchman if you are not polite. Courtesy is a must. As children they are constantly told, *soyez toujour polite*. In other words, regardless of circumstances a person should always be polite."

Melissa said, "That's probably the better way."

After finishing a bite of the baguette she asked, "Where are you all from? I can tell you are not Americans."

"We are from Belfast. Rosheen teaches French and I speak the language too. We fit in well here. At least better here than in many other countries. We like France and come here every few years on holidays. We spend time in Paris and try to see at least one different castle each time."

Macarten looked at his watch.

"Oh, I didn't realize it. It's getting late. If we want to catch the bus we had better be moving along. If you will excuse us we must go to our room. We need to freshen up a bit and retrieve a few items. We will look for you on the bus."

Melissa said, "Oh, ok. By the way, where are we going today?"

"Chateau Fontainebleau. It's a lovely castle. We've been told the gardens and the interiors are definitely worth seeing. This is one of the castles we have not seen as yet. So, we're looking forward to the excursion."

"Oh, I see. Well, if I can get my husband moving we will see you on the bus."

"Later then."

Macarten and Rosheen Maldonan took their leave of Melissa and walked toward the stairs that led to the floor above.

Melissa finished her breakfast and returned to Room 322. Mark was dressed and sitting at a desk with his head in his hands.

"We have to get moving darling. The bus is scheduled to leave in about fifteen minutes. Don't forget your camera."

"I'm as ready as I will ever be. Where is the tour bus going today?"

"A castle by the name of Fontainebleau. A couple in the lobby told me. I guess it was on the brochure we have somewhere. They'll be on the bus."

The tour of the castle and grounds lasted about an hour. Mark took thirty-five photos with his Nikon digital camera. The photos were intended for showing to friends, neighbors and their daughters. Basically, an opportunity to brag. After walking around the castle grounds everyone climbed back on the bus. It was lunchtime and according to the agenda the driver took the assembly to a nearby restaurant by the name of *Chez Bernard*. Before the driver opened the bus door in the restaurant parking lot he announced that the group will be here for two hours or, if needed, longer.

Mark whispered to his wife, "Two hours. Why two hours?"

At the door of his restaurant, Bernard Larue, owner of the

restaurant, personally greeted the tourists and welcomed them into his establishment. Melissa and Mark were the last to descend from the bus. Inside the restaurant, Rosheen and Macarten were already seated near a window that overlooked a well manicured flower garden. Macarten waved them over and gestured toward the two empty seats at the table. As Melissa and Mark approached, Macarten stood and extended his hand in the direction of Mark.

"I'm Macarten Maldonan."

They shook hands. Macarten added, "We met your wife this morning at the hotel. Wont you have a seat?"

Mark said, "Yeah, sure. I need a seat."

Before taking a seat, Mark hung his camera bag on the back of his chair.

Mark looked at both Melissa and Mark and asked, "Did you enjoy the tour of the chateau, Mark?"

Mark answered, "Yeah, I guess. Boy, those kings sure lived high on the hog in their day."

Macarten nodded, suggesting agreement.

"You are certainly right there. Fontainebleau is one of the few castles where the furnishings survived the revolution. The chairs, tables and tapestries that we saw were the same that were seen and used by the king and the queen and later by Napoleon and Josephine."

Melissa added her impression.

"If I were queen, I would be outside in those gardens most of the day. I would tell my servants to cut that flower for me and that one over there, too. Bring them to our bedroom. Keep some for the dining room table. I'd have a good old time prancing around, giving orders right and left. Wouldn't that be fun, Rosheen?"

"Oh, indeed. Great fun. As queen I would also spend the morning in the gardens. Later I would be off riding horseback on a great white stallion. Behind me I would have my entourage, also on horseback, waiting for the snap of my fingers. Every now and then I would bring everything to a halt and declare a glass of sherry for all. By the time we returned to the stables, everyone would be in a good mood and loving their gracious queen."

Everyone laughed.

A waitress appeared with a pad in her hand.

"Monsieur, madam! Would you like something to drink. Perhaps an apéritif or some wine?"

Macarten looked at Rosheen. Rosheen decided to speak first.

"*D'accord, madam. Une dubonet ici.*"

Macarten followed.

"*La meme, si vous plait.*"

Melissa asked, "Do you have Coca Cola?"

"No, sorry. Perhaps you would prefer a Perrier?"

"Yes, that will work."

Mark was the last to order.

"I'll have a beer but not if it's warm. I'm not drinking anymore warm beer."

As her English was limited, the waitress did not entirely understand the order.

Rosheen explained.

"*Le monsieur demande de bière à la pression mai soulment si il est froide. Pa du bière chaude.*"

"*Je comprende. Une bière à la pression froide pour le monsieur.*"

The drinks were served and enjoyed by all. Mark started to feel better. A second round was ordered and likewise enjoyed. After the drinks it was time to order the entrées. Rosheen explained that in France entrées are what in Britain are called starters and not the main course. Rosheen ordered oysters on the half shell and Macarten ordered snails. Both Melissa and

Mark chose salads. When the snails and raw oysters arrived Melissa excused herself for a visit to the washroom. After she returned to the table she tried to avoid looking at the snails or oysters. Rosheen suggested that they order a bottle of white and a bottle of red. When the waitress returned, the two bottles were ordered.

For the main course Rosheen ordered sole meuniere and Macarten poulet roti. Melissa asked for a hamburger but the waitress said she was sorry. With a raised nose the waitress said hamburgers were not served in the restaurant. She noted that there are McDonald's in Paris and that Melissa might like to visit one of them the next time she is in the vicinity. Melissa, taken aback, declared she did not like greasy French food and told the waitress she will merely have a bowl of soup. Mark said he would like a sirloin steak, well cooked, and a baked potato but settled for bifteck au poivre with mashed potatoes.

When the waitress was out of earshot Melissa spoke first, looking at the Brits.

"Can you imagine that? A restaurant that doesn't serve hamburgers. In America every restaurant serves hamburgers. Mark and I like hamburgers."

The courses were delivered in stages with the result that at times one person would be eating while three people watched. Melissa said she didn't know why the meals took so long.

"And why were they not served all at the same time. You would think the cooks would plan a little better."

Rosheen explained this was the French way. Better to have a well prepared dish than one that is scheduled to appear with another one. Near the end of the two-hour lunch all had coffee.

After the bus arrived at the hotel on the return trip the two couples gathered in the lobby. Macarten shook hands with Mark and said that if he and Melissa were ever in Belfast to please look them up. He added that Rosheen and he will be taking the train to London that evening. Mark said likewise, namely that if Macarten and Rosheen are in Butler someday.

Taking the stairs to their room, Macarten commented, "Interesting couple."

In the elevator, Mark said he thought the British couple were, "very friendly." Melissa answered, "Yes, I guess so. I just wish they wouldn't have ordered those ugly snails and oysters the way they did. So disgusting. Tomorrow we are going to find a McDonalds somewhere."

The Two Mile Club
(A creative nonfiction short story)

Alan Keene, a guard at the Brendon Heights Nuclear Plant, was trying his best to stay awake. Despite his best efforts, now and then his eyelids closed and his head bobbed forward. Alan's assignment for that day was to watch the plant's closed circuit TV monitors. The monitors provided a means whereby the guards can watch for suspicious activity at the outer fence and selected locations within the plant. It was a boring assignment, and most guards would say that they would generally prefer doing something different. However, that particular day with an outside temperature somewhere below fifteen degrees Fahrenheit and a wind above twenty miles an hour, Alan was pleased to be sitting on a comfortable chair in a warm room. If only he could manage to stay awake.

A little after midnight another of the plant's guards, Hunter Rollins, stepped out of the cold for a chat. He had been walking a beat around the plant's facilities.

"Staying awake, Alan?"

"Yeah, I am. But it's tough at times. That gallon of coffee helped."

"I'd gladly trade places with you tonight. Believe me, it's brutal out there. Walking from the Intake Structure to the Engineering Building I thought the wind was going to blow me into the fence. I'll tell you I am glad I put on my long John's."

"Hunter, working a few chilly nights per year won't hurt

you. Being paid to mostly go for a walk is easy money, good money. And you know it.”

“I won’t argue with you there. This job is one hell of a lot better than pushing a wheelbarrow or laying bricks.”

The two guards exchange thoughts for a spell while Hunter rubbed his hands and tried to warm up. After a time, Alan’s visitor zipped his jacket closed and replaced his gloves.

“Have to get on the beat again. Stay awake. The supers get especially upset if they find a sleeping guard. I heard of one guy who was caught dozing. It was the second time apparently. He was told on the spot to get his things, turn in his badge and don’t plan on coming back to the plant.”

Hunter forced the exit door open against the wind and disappeared into the night. Alan returned his attention to the monitors. All was quiet for a spell, and his eyelids once more grew heavy. After a few head bobs the sound of a bell startled Alan. A motion detector had sensed movement where none was expected. Two of the monitors had automatically flashed to scenes in the office of Plant Manager Mr. Thompson. At first, Alan thought there must be something amiss with the system. Perhaps a mouse ran across the floor and triggered the alarm. That happened frequently. The plant manager’s office was in the Administration Building and after midnight there should be no activity in that building. Peering at the monitor, it became apparent that the lights in the office were on. Also strange.

Leaning forward to position his head closer to the monitor, Alan was surprised to see people moving around in the office. In fact there were two persons, a man and a woman. And, both were in the process of undressing. Alan did not wait. He pressed the button for channel number one on the security radio. That immediately put him in communication with all of the plant’s guards.

“This is Alan Keene in the Security Center. Is anyone near

the Admin Building?"

Guard Justin Bradley turned his two-way radio to "transmit."

"This is Bradley. I'm in the Access Building. Mason Lorah and me are here warming up for a little. Trying to avoid frostbite."

"Justin, I need you to investigate Mr. Thompson's office in the Admin Building, Room 137. There are two unauthorized persons there. Tell them to put their clothes back on and return to wherever it is they belong."

Justin Bradley turned to face Mason while answering Alan's call.

"What do you mean, put their clothes on?"

"I don't have time to chew the fat. If you don't double time there you might miss them. I don't know how long they will be at it. Get moving. Be polite. Don't get rough with anyone. Be sure to get their names and badge numbers. Just do your job and you will live to collect another paycheck."

Justin answered, "Ten-forty. We're on our way."

Alan was not a supervisor and had no authority to give orders to other guards. The guards of the Security Department were not organized as, say, a police force where there is a hierarchy of uppers and lowers, corporals, sergeants and the like. Nevertheless, Alan's fellow guards tended to regard Alan as something of a father figure. He was older than most of the guards and had ample on-the-job experience. He was inclined to give worthwhile advice to those who conducted themselves in a respectful and conscientious manner. If Alan suggests that a guard do this or that, Alan's words were generally taken as solid advice and usually followed.

Justin grabbed his rifle and stood up.

"Ok, sport, put on your gloves. Let's go to the Admin Building to see who doesn't have their clothes on. This should be interesting."

Alan continued to watch the monitor. He plainly saw the nude couple displayed on the monitor carefully remove every article from the desk in the office and carry each item over to an adjacent table. They did not seem to be in a hurry. Next the woman lay on the executive's desk, belly up, and waiting. The camera in the eastern wall showed the man as he approached the desk where his girlfriend for the evening waited. Alan did not like the profile displayed from the eastern camera and switched to the camera on the northern wall. The man climbed up on the desk and proceeded to do his part.

***

Sometime after the episode in the plant manager's office, Justin Bradley and Mason Lorah strolled into the Security Center. Mason displayed a broad smile and ten nicotine-stained teeth.

Coming close Justin told Alan, "That was some scene. I never saw anything like that."

"Justin, living far out in the country as you do there are a lot of things you haven't seen. Did you get their names?"

"The girl is Lindsey Benning, a clerk from the Refueling Department. One hot chick! You should have seen the tattoos on her butt."

"What about the guy?"

"Who was looking at him?"

"The name, Justin. I'm talking about the name. Did you get his name like you're supposed to do?"

"The guy is an electrical tech, name of Ben Rexnard."

"Write up your report. You can use the computer over there in the corner. I'll let the super know about the incident. He can take it from there. I hope the copulators didn't leave the office in a mess."

"Oh, no. Not at all. They put everything back exactly the

way they found it. We stayed around to be sure they straightened up. Mr. Thompson won't be able to see any difference when he comes to his office in the morning."

Alan smiled and declared, "Good. It seems you handled it the right way. I'll send an email to Larry Hasley to let him know what happened in Thompson's office. I'll mention that the cameras gave us a clear and complete recording of the intrusion."

Minutes after Alan sent the email, Larry Hasley, unsmiling, appeared at Alan's desk.

"Who was the guard who responded to that intrusion into Mr. Thompson's office?"

"That would be Justin Bradley."

"Did he write up his report?"

"He said he would. I think he did. I saw him use the computer terminal over there in the corner."

"Get me a hard copy of the report. Call Rexnard and have him report to my office at 3 a.m."

"Yes, sir."

***

As requested, Ben Rexnard reported to Larry Hasley's office at 3 a.m. After Ben entered, Larry walked over and gently closed the door.

"Have a seat, Ben."

Ben shuffled over and slouched down in the chair in front of Larry's desk. He was wearing his usual blue jeans, a tee shirt and white sneakers. Ben did not have the appearance of an intellectual, one who would be reading books on the best sellers list. He seemed more like the kind of guy who would be happy in the evenings with a beer in one hand and the TV remote in the other. An easy-going type and with looks the women might notice.

Slowly, Larry walked behind his desk and took a seat.

Looking Ben in the eye, he asked, "Work hard last night, Ben?"

"Oh, yes. I was busy making up a list of needed transmitters. Some of them are approaching the end of their allowable lifetimes and I need to order replacements. I did take a couple of coffee breaks though. I'm always sleepy the first few nights when I first start on the graveyard shift. It takes a few days until my system adjusts. After a day or two I'll be ok."

"Coffee breaks I can understand, Ben. What about sex breaks, Ben? Take any sex breaks last night?"

Ben concentrated on his shoes. He realized it was time to be humble and extra careful with what he said. One wrong word and he could be out on the street without a job. He suspected he might be headed there anyway. He realized Larry knew about the little tryst with his secret girlfriend. He decided it would be best to say nothing more on the subject for the moment.

"Look, Ben. Just tell me the truth here and I think all will be fine. Otherwise, I can't make any promises. We all know boys will be boys and mischief will follow. Please let me know, though! If you are going to diddle some chick at the plant and on company time, why must you choose to do it on the plant manager's desk of all places?"

Ben hesitated but was aware he must be straightforward. All things equal he would prefer to keep his job. He knew that being fired at a nuclear plant would most likely prevent employment at another nuclear plant anywhere in the world. He was likewise aware that the people who operate these plants keep databases for a long time and they exchange critical information about employees. Besides, pay at the plant was better than what could be found elsewhere in the area.

Ben replied, "I'll be honest. Have you ever heard of the Mile High Club?"

"No, I don't think that I have."

"Well, it is not really a club at all. Couples who have sex in an airplane can say they are members of the Mile High Club. Some couples find it a challenge. Something different, you know. Mostly they do it in the restroom of a commercial flight going from city A to city B. You can read all about the Mile High Club on the Internet. It's well known in certain circles. Of course anyone can say they did it in an airplane. Neither proof nor witnesses are required. Anyway, some of my old school buddies in town got the idea to start a similar club. It might be because none of them travel much in airplanes. They call their club the Two Mile Club.

The local Two Mile Club is more or less the workingman's Mile High Club. The motto of the Two Mile Club is that, 'We go the extra mile.' Just like the Mile High Club it's also not a true club. Anyone can say they are a member. So far it's been only men at the annual meetings. The group has grown in the last few years. At the last meeting, twenty-four guys showed up. The meetings are held once a year on the day of the Army-Navy game. That way it's easy to remember the date. We drink a lot of beer, eat some wings, listen to stories and assign points. Some guys just come to the meetings to drink beer and listen to the stories."

Ben stopped. He was uncertain how much more would be of interest to Larry.

Larry looked at the ceiling, much as in disbelief. He encouraged Ben to, "Go on."

"One of the organizers wrote up what he calls the rules for membership. According to the rules, to become a bona fide member a guy must have sex in some unusual way. However, sex in an airplane doesn't count. There are guys who have said they have done it on horseback, in a canoe, rock climbing, under water. The list goes on. Points are assigned for originality, but no event gets more than ten points. There are no points for a repeat performance, but copying another guy's method is ok. One guy has fifty-five points. Of course there is no proof of any reported episode. The club's secretary keeps a record."

"Look, Ben. I've heard enough. Can I assume there will be no further efforts on your part to earn points for the Two Mile Club on company time or on company property? Can I also assume you will make no mention of this tryst to anybody? I see no need for Mr. Thompson to be concerned with events of this type. He has enough on his mind trying to run this plant. So, if he thinks everything was normal last night, well, that should keep everyone happy. And I don't want the union complaining about too many cameras around the plant. We get enough trouble from them as it is. As far as your little cutie goes, well, I will assume you can persuade her to also keep quiet."

Ben appeared relieved as he replied, "You have my word."

"Fine! If you keep your word, I believe you can keep your job. However, Human Resources has the final word on that. Later today I will advise your super and I suspect there will be a letter of reprimand. But I suspect that should be the extent of it. Now, please return to your work site."

Ben stood up and meekly exited the room. Back in the Electrical Department he checked his emails. No new emails. Looking around to confirm that there was nobody within earshot he called Lindsey.

"Hi, sweetheart. It's me."

"I am so embarrassed, Ben. That guard walking in on us the way he did. Do you think he will tell anyone? Is there any need for me to tell you that I am not doing that or anything like it again? Ever. You and your God-damned Two Mile Club. What a stupid idea."

"Lindsey, believe me I am sorry, really sorry, about what happened. Listen, there is something I need to tell you. One of the security bosses called me into his office. He knew about our little session. I suspect that security has hidden cameras in that office. That's how they knew we were there. Who would've known they had cameras in the plant manager's office? Anyhow, I think that is how they came to know we were there. If they have cameras there, then the whole event was probably recorded."

"What? Ben, what are you saying? That there is a recording somewhere of what we were doing in that office? Ben, this is terrible. What if my husband hears about this?"

"I don't know for sure that there is a recording. It's only something that I suspect. The super told me that if I keep quiet about this event, I can most likely keep my job. I think the same applies to you. He told me they would like to keep things like this to themselves. He said that if I don't go around talking to others about this, then everything should be alright. That is what I intend to do. I think that if we both keep this quiet we will both be ok. I just wanted you to know what he told me."

"Ben, this is disgusting. Of course I am not going to be running around telling people that I had sex with Ben Rexnard on the plant manager's desk. Oh, Jane, would you like a DVD of me and Ben screwing on the plant manager's desk. It's such a gas. Show it to your friends. You must take me to be dumber than I look. I have to get back to work."

She slammed the handset into its cradle.

That day Ben's supervisor was advised of the event. A letter of reprimand was sent to Ben in a few days and a copy was placed in his electronic folder at Human Resources. For some reason, no reprimand was sent to Lindsey. Neither Lindsey nor Ben told another person about what happened that cold night on the plant manager's desk at the Brendon Heights Nuclear Plant. Plant Manager Michael Thompson never learned of the incursion into his office.

***

Alan Keene's replacement at the Security console, Stan Patyanoski, showed up fifteen minutes before the start of his shift.

"Hi, Stan. You're early."

"Yes. What with the weather as it is, it's better to allow a little extra travel time. You know being late for work does not help the record. Boy, I'm glad to have a desk assignment tonight. It's not a good night to be walking around out there."

"Stan, I'll be leaving in a few minutes. It will be all yours. Look, if you get bored during the night there is something that might keep you awake for a spell. It's one of the recordings."

"What? One of the cameras caught a raccoon trying to climb the fence. Or, was it two deer making love outside the fence?"

"You are not far wrong. Listen, when you're alone in the center tonight and you need something to keep you awake, call up the recording for Room 137 starting at 1:05 a.m."

"Room 137. Isn't that Thompson's office?"

"Yes. Just keep yourself whatever you see. The bosses don't want this spread around."

"If you say so. I'll do it."

***

When Plant Manager Michael Thompson walked into his office the day after the early morning intrusion he noticed that the telephone was not where he had last seen it. Being left-handed, he preferred that the telephone to be positioned on the right side of the desk. That way, he could hold the handset with his right hand while he wrote with his left hand. When he had calls, he would place the telephone on "speaker". But, if there were people in his office he would use the handset. He wondered what might have happened. He decided it must have been the cleaning lady who moved it. Strange, though, he thought. That never happened before.

Later in the day when Michael Thompson bent down to tie a shoe lace, he spotted a woman's earring under his desk. He figured that too could be attributed to the cleaning lady. He fetched the ear ring and placed it on a piece of paper where he suspected the cleaning lady would more readily spot it.

Ben attended the annual meeting of the Two Mile Club the evening of the Army-Navy game. Before the meeting, he had resolved to himself that no matter how much beer he might have under his belt that night, he was not going to mention the tryst on the Plant Manager's desk. Having a little fun with a part-time girlfriend at the plant was one thing. Losing a job, a wife and a place to stay would be an entirely different matter. As usual, he enjoyed listening to the stories of others at the meeting. There were eight men who made claims and a total of sixty-three points were awarded. Three were registered as new members. Of course, Ben downed his normal volume of beer and ate his share of wings. He wanted to be sure he got his rightful share for the twenty dollars attendance fee he had paid.

Near the end of the annual meeting of the club one of the regulars seated near Ben noted Ben's unusual silence.

"Hey, Ben, you aren't saying much tonight. No points this year?"

"No, not this year. It's been a real busy year at the plant. No time for extracurricular activities. Maybe next year though. We'll see."

The Late Train from Alexandria
(A creative nonfiction short story)

I should have known better than to take the late train. Although I had been cautioned, I chose to disregard the well-intended advice. Once aboard and underway, everything seemed normal. But, the farther the train traveled the greater my apprehension.

That day I had visited our business associate, El Seoud Engineering, in Alexandria. The visit was only one of many I had made to their office in the heart of the ancient city. Usually I would exit the train at the eastern station, the Sida Gaber Station, and from there walk some five blocks through back streets. The alternative was to wait until the end of the line, which was at the Mahattat Misr station, and take a taxi from there to the El Seoud offices. That route required more time and, I had learned, more complications. The walk along the back streets took much less time, and it was more interesting, but there was also reason for caution. A variety of people could typically be seen along the way. Some were well dressed, obviously prosperous and most likely well-intended. Others seemed to be permanent residents of the streets and wearing rags for clothing, desperate individuals with no regular source of food or shelter. People who, it might be suspected, might try anything to extend their survival.

The people of Egypt are a mix of cultures, civilizations and classes. Many have a Western appearance whereas others dress in the traditional Arab garb. Many women wear a scarf over their hair but most do not. Some people are swarthy whereas others are as fair skinned as European. Many speak English. Yet, beneath the widespread appearances of civility, a few individuals harbor a hatred for foreigners, their ways and their beliefs. Given an opportunity, those miscreants would turn their dark convictions into hateful and violent action.

When I arrived at the El Seoud offices that morning I pushed my way through the front door. The secretary greeted me with a, "Good morning, Mr. Fleckenstein. Welcome back to Alexandria. We were expecting you."

She was an attractive young woman with dark brown eyes, lovely black hair and a pleasant, ready smile. I had seen her in the same office on previous visits. I told her, "Good morning. I must say I anticipated somewhat more comfortable temperatures."

"Sorry for that, sir. Unlike Cairo, this time of the year the air can be chilly in Alexandria. Perhaps we will have better conditions for your next visit. Try to visit us in the spring or fall. You will find the weather at that time of the year more pleasant. May I assume you are here to see Mr. Ramallah?"

"Yes, is he about?"

"I will fetch him for you."

True to form, the receptionist appeared with Khalid Ramallah in a few minutes. He told me, "Good morning, Mr. Fleckenstein. Good to see you again. Did you have a pleasant trip?"

"Yes, thank you," I told him. "The trip was event-free which, of course, is the best kind. Good morning to you."

"Please come back to my office. Would you like tea?"

"Tea would be fine, thank you."

Khalid led me to a seat in his office, and then he went looking for the office boy. When he returned, we discussed the weather, tourists and other innocuous subjects. In time, the office boy appeared with tea. As was typical in Arab countries, the tea was served in cups that were slightly larger than Western whiskey glasses. I could have easily handled a dozen of them, but I declined a second offering. Moderation and courtesies were important. Our discussion slowly turned to business matters. We spent the remainder of the morning reviewing drawings, contracts and project progress.

Lunch was always an event to anticipate. On every previous visit, I had been taken to fine restaurants and one that would be different from the last one we visited. Once we went to what was at one time the palace of the last king of Egypt, King Farouk. Dining in a room that had been converted to a private restaurant, my hosts and I enjoyed a meal of seafood while overlooking the blue Mediterranean. Later, we went for a stroll on some of the 365 streets that had been constructed on the palace grounds solely for the king's promenading pleasure.

Khalid Ramallah and I returned to the office after lunch and continued our business discussions. Generally our business matters had been settled in time so that I could take one of the afternoon express trains for the return trip to Cairo where I had a room in a hotel. In fact, Khalid had recommended that on that day I should take one of the afternoon trains. On more than one occasion in the past he had told me something similar to what he said that day: "Mr. Fleckenstein, you should avoid taking the evening train to Cairo. You will find one of the earlier trains more to your liking."

No further explanation was rendered regarding train schedules. Khalid's comments often led me to wonder what could possibly be wrong with a late train. Regardless, I was disinclined to inquire. In my dealings with foreigners I learned to minimize questions. Whereas many Americans will verbalize questions that pop into their heads, people from many other countries do not welcome direct questions.

Khalid typically resolved the travel arrangements by providing me with an express train ticket in advance of my departing. The train ticket was procured by sending the office boy to the station in advance of my departure. The advanced purchase ensured that I would be taking one of the express trains to Cairo and, in addition, that I would have a seat in a first class coach.

The day I took the late train from Alexandria there were too many drawings that required my attention. The effort could not be completed satisfactorily before El Seoud's normal quitting time. I hoped to avoid returning again the following day from Cairo since the unresolved matters would require no more than two hours time. Consequently, I stayed until late. Since the office boy had been allowed to go home I would be obliged to go to the main station and purchase a ticket.

By 7:35 p.m. my effort was finally completed, and Khalid saw me to the door. He wished me the usual, "Assalam."

I returned an "Assalam."

I was uncertain of the meaning although I expected it was some sort of parting good wishes that suited the occasion.

Walking in the general direction of the train station, and distracted by my thoughts of the project, I somehow made a wrong turn. I realized I was lost. Some street people noticed my predicament. An older, bearded man sitting on the steps ahead seemed to take particular interest in me. As he started to rise, I quickly changed direction. I did not have time to deal with beggars. Fortunately, I spotted a well-dressed man coming in the opposite direction. From a distance it seemed he might be friendly. Approaching him, I asked for directions.

"Excuse me, sir, could you direct me to the Misr Station?"

"Yes," he told me. "You are going completely in the wrong direction. The Misr Station. It is over this way."

He pointed to my left.

"Go straight to El-maamoun Street then left. Another two or three streets. You will see the station."

I thanked the man, hoping that his directions would help me find the station before my train departed. With the sun down, the evening air was turning chilly. I was glad to be wearing a jacket although it was not nearly enough. I looked forward to the warmer air in Cairo.

When I arrived at the station, the large clock near the platforms showed the time to be a few minutes before 8:00 p.m. All of the ticket windows had long lines of people waiting to make their purchases. It started to appear doubtful that I would make the 8:00 p.m. train. Soldiers were everywhere, rifles slung over their shoulders, watching for troublemakers. Half of the eligible men in Egypt must be in the army. When the station clock showed 8:00 p.m. there were still three people in front of me at the ticket window. Fortunately they all purchased their tickets without questions and soon it was my turn.

The clerk asked me, "How many tickets?"

I told him, "One first class ticket on the train to Cairo."

"No more first class tickets on the eight o'clock train. Only second class. Do you want second class ticket?"

I knew that second class cars had no air conditioning, only hard seats and questionable travel companions. I hesitated and the ticket agent became impatient. I concluded I had little choice in the matter. Offhand I was uncertain when the next rain would be departing. It might be hours away and, furthermore, it might likewise have no first class seats. I decided to go with a second class ticket on the 8:00 p.m. train.

I told the man, "Yes, one second class ticket, please."

"Fifteen pounds."

I placed fifteen pounds, Egyptian, on the counter. The agent took the money without a word and gave me a ticket on a train to Cairo.

I asked, "Where is the train, please?"

"Track two. Next person."

According to the station clock, the time was after 8:00 p.m., but I was uncertain as to which track was Track Number Two. I saw no sign that identified the tracks. There were several trains in the station. All posted information in the stations was in Arabic although most signs also had an English translation. I needed to quickly find both the correct train as well as the second class coaches.

I walked toward a waiting train that I thought might be on Track Number Two. Ahead, I spotted a man entering a coach on the train. He climbed the steps to one of the better coaches. Farther down the platform I saw other coaches that appeared to be more rustic and in need of paint. I guessed they were the second class coaches. Hurriedly, I made my way along the platform. I expected the train to start moving any moment. I hurried aboard the nearest coach. Inside the air was hot and full of a variety of odors. The seats were elementary and generally tattered. The occupants appeared to be other than prosperous. The first coach I entered was full, every seat taken, so I continued through it to the next one.

The second car was almost full, but I found a seat near a window. A few more passengers entered the car. One was a man with his tongue fully extended. His tongue went out and curved down to his chin. He withdrew it periodically but it quickly snapped back to the extended position. Poor fellow. He could not keep the thing in his mouth. I had never seen a similar malady. I avoided staring at the strange scene.

Much to my benefit the train was late to depart. The engineer sounded the locomotive's horn and the train jerked forward. I assumed the train was heading for the Ramses Station in Cairo. Allowing my head to fall back against the headrest, my eye lids grew heavy. It had been a long day. I expected that in roughly two hours' time the train would arrive in Cairo and I would be heading toward my hotel. There, I hoped to find a beer, supper and a rest. I felt I needed those things, earned them actually.

Sleep came easily, but then, startled, I sensed someone quietly slip into the seat next to me. With a side-glance I saw the person to be a mustachioed man in traditional Arab dress. His skin was weathered much like that of the desert people, the Bedouin, and unlike that of the city-dwellers. He was not carrying a thing. A rough looking man! Looking at me he said a few words in Arabic. I nodded but said nothing. I did not wish to have him peg me as a foreigner and a worthwhile target! Better rude than robbed or dead! Others, I noticed, were watching him. For some reason, the man warranted their attention. Suddenly, I was no longer sleepy. After a few minutes reflection, I told myself I should not be so alarmed. I tried sleep again but with no success.

After several miles the train slowed and then halted again. Looking through the window I saw we were at a stop, albeit a small one. A few, new passengers boarded, and the train continued its travel.

In another five minutes, the train slowed to a second stop. A small assembly was waiting on the platform to come aboard. The group included a Muslim family, complete with father, mother and two small girls. The man of the family was wearing a white keffiyeh headdress and a brown Arab thawb that went to his ankles. He was a handsome man who stood erect, apparently proud of his family. He stood with that enviable posture characteristic of many of the Arab men. His neck went straight up and his head was held aloof. The wife's features were hidden behind a black burga that went from the top of her head to the soles of her shoes. A pair of eyes, long ago subdued, could be seen peering out of a narrow slot in the garment. The girls were still, standing safely by their mother's side.

A middle-aged couple, in Western dress, stood a few feet behind the Muslim family. The man wore a white shirt and trousers, she a calf length dress and a yellow blouse. Her hair was uncovered. Their skins were more white than brown. They could have been European tourists, secular Muslims or Coptic Christians. There was no telling which. Part of the mix and mystery of Egypt! Quickly the people from the platform boarded, and the train resumed its forward movement. The Bedouin beside me, apparently harmless, fell asleep.

As the train eased its way through the countryside, periodic reflections of the moon could be seen off the water of the irrigation canals. On a prior trip I had seen nude boys swimming and frolicking in those canals, canals that held a dark water channeled from the Nile River. The river that made life possible in Egypt.

In what seemed to be an unreasonably short time, the train stopped again. The station platform at this stop was relatively small. Looking out the window, I saw a shoeless man, not thirty feet away, sitting on a building's stoop. He probably lived in the building behind him, perhaps along with many others. If he lived in America he would be watching TV or fiddling with an electronic gadget of some type. In that man's his predicament, however, none of these activities were an option. If, somehow, he came onto possession of any of these devices he would have no use for them. There would be no electricity in the house to activate the TV or to recharge batteries.

Egypt, I learned, had tens of thousands of abandoned houses. Those houses have no water or electricity but most are occupied with squatters. They are the result of an old law that limits increases in the rent. With inflation, the owners no longer found reason to maintain the properties. Most likely the shoeless man lived in one of those properties.

The train continued on its way. As it slowed again for the next stop, the man with the extended tongue stood to gather his belongings. He moved to the door in preparation for exiting the coach. A dozen or so Egyptians were on the platform, waiting to board. At that stop, most were in Arab dress. A few were young men, the type that could be malcontents and serious fanatics.

The passengers came aboard and the train again resumed its forward movement. It made another fifteen or more stops. I lost count. I did not recognize any of the stops, and I could not remember having seen any of them on the many prior trips I had made to and from Alexandria. I was beginning to suspect we were on a different track. I began to have serious concerns. Could it be that we were taking a different route to Cairo? Was the train actually heading for Cairo? In the past, all of my trips were by express trains and only a matter of two hours more or less. Yet, we had been travelling almost three hours. Did I actually take the train to Cairo—or had I misunderstood the signs at the station and inadvertently boarded one headed to a destination other than Cairo?

True, I thought, a non-express would take more time. I wondered if we had already passed through Cairo and I failed to recognize the stop? It occurred to me that perhaps the train was going to a small village somewhere in the Eastern Desert, a village where no English was spoken. If so, I would become a natural target. A lone Westerner who would be suspected of having money in his pocket…a non-believer. I would have no way to return to Cairo. Late at night there would be no taxis or busses. I had not seen a conductor for hours, and there was no one to ask. As the travel time exceeded three hours, my concerns became troubling. It also occurred to me that the train might be on its way to Suez or Port Said.

I sensed movement to my left and turned to see the

Bedouin stand. He glanced at me as he turned to walk to the rear of the car. Perhaps it was a coincident! Within seconds, an Egyptian soldier, rifle between his hands, entered the front door of the coach. I wondered if he was searching for someone in particular, or merely looking for potential trouble? Shortly he continued walking through to the coach at the rear, essentially in the footsteps of the Bedouin.

The train gradually entered a slight bend that curved to the left. Through the window to the right I saw lights ahead. The illumination was obviously from a large town or a city. I hoped it was Cairo. *Please*, I thought, *let it be Cairo*. Everyone in the car stood to claim their belongings as the train was obviously coming to the termination point of its travel. When the train slowed I saw a most wonderful sight out the window: a sign with Arabic writing as well as the English words "Cairo - Ramses Station. I gave a sigh of relief.

Without delay I found a taxi and told the driver, "Zamalek Hotel." I sorely needed a beer.

The Annual Turkey Calling Contest
(A creative nonfiction short story)

Turkey calling contests are a big deal in some circles. Some call manufacturers, with the hope of improving product sales, send proven callers to enter the contests. Others enter merely for the enjoyment and the potential bragging rights. People come from far-away places to watch and to participate. Typically, the attendees are from those areas where wild turkeys live in abundance. Texas, Florida and Wyoming send more than what seems to be their fair share of contestants.

Turkey calling contests are commonly held in conjunction with hunting sports shows. The shows are usually staged in January or February. It's considered an appropriate time of the year because the fall hunting seasons have closed and the spring gobbler seasons have yet to begin..

I had been hunting and calling turkeys for many years, both in the fall and in the spring. Maybe I should explain! Many of the states that have turkey hunting will have a fall season in addition to the spring hunt. Moreover, there are several calls that a hunter may use to call a turkey to the position where he waits with shogun at the ready. The calls used in the fall are different from those used in the spring. The real sport is in the spring when the turkeys are mating. To harvest a gobbler at that time of the year, a hunter will imitate the mating call of the hen. If the call is a good simulation of a real and sexy hen, the gobbler may come over to investigate. At least, that is what is intended. However, gobblers are smart and suspicious by nature. In nature, it's the hen that normally travels to the gobbler for a tryst. So, asking a gobbler to come to a caller is against the bird's nature. Most often, the gobbler will respond with a gobble, thereby inviting the hen to a get-together. Yet, a gobbler will travel to the source of a call it believes is emanating from a serious hen.

Hunters use a variety of calls to entice a gobbler. Three of the more popular calls are the box, the slate and the diaphragm. The box call and the slate call are operated with hands, and that feature can pose problems. When a turkey is nearby, the hunter needs to stop using the call and switch to his or her gun. That's motion a sharp turkey may spot. The diaphragm call is used in the mouth of the hunter, and, so, this minimizes motion when a turkey is near. My preference is the slate call for the reason that I have had better success with it, although at times I would also use a diaphragm call. If I am using a slate call, I will switch to a diaphragm call when a turkey approaches. I thought I had become proficient with the diaphragm call, and that is what prompted me to try my luck at one of the annual calling contests.

When I went to my first contest, I wore my usual jeans and a flannel shirt. Some of the contestants really were into the spirt of the moment with their head-to-toe camo outfits. Just like they would dress when entering the woods on a serious hunt, except for a face mask. I didn't see any face masks. Inside the arena, people were making turkey calls in every corner, both warming up and celebrating the event. At the registration desk, a young lady asked me to sign a roster and she gave me a slip of paper with the number twenty-five written on it. Smiling, she told me, "When your number is called, just go over to the booth and start calling. You can do as many calls as you like, as long as you include a yelp and a purr."

The show was scheduled to start in half an hour after I arrived. Around three dozen people milled around the area. Mostly there were groups of twos and threes. A few singles, too, like myself. I found a seat next to a young man who seemed to also be alone. He was about my age. I asked him if he had done this before. He said, "No, first time. What about you?" I told him I had watched contests before but that I had never participated. We got to talking about turkey hunting. He told me he lived nearby and he too was an avid turkey hunter. His name was Mason Heim. We shook hands. I asked him if he was going to use a diaphragm call. He said they all do.

At three in the afternoon a man standing near the registration desk announced the competition was to begin. Without further explanation, he called out "number fifteen." Apparently the contestants were being called in random order. A tall guy wearing western boots and a camo baseball cap stood and walked slowly to the calling booth. He obviously intended the walk to inform all observers that he knew what he was doing. A movable partition that was about seven feet tall separated the caller from the judges. The judges could hear the calls but they couldn't see the contestants.

Number fifteen put a diaphragm call in his mouth and immediately did a fly down cackle. He followed with the yelp and then a purr. The calls sounded genuine to me. If I had closed my eyes, I could have sworn there was a live turkey nearby. I didn't think anyone could have done better. Number fifteen returned to his seat where another man spoke softly to him. I suspected number fifteen's friend was complimenting him on his performance.

The next caller was number twenty-one. His performance was less than mediocre. In my opinion, he never would have been able to call a gobbler to his position with calls of the type he demonstrated. He shook his head as he returned to his seat. He knew he hadn't done well. Maybe it was his nerves.

When my number was called, I stepped to the booth and withdrew my diaphragm call. I must admit, I had a touch of stage fright. First, I did the required yelp and purr. I followed those with a cluck and a cut. I was pleased with myself, although I knew I was not going to place in the top three. The official called Mason later, and I thought he did alright.

After two hours of calling, an official of the event declared the contest at an end. The three judges came around to show their faces and to shake hands with people they knew from past encounters. The young lady behind the registration table stood and announced, "The winner of today's contest had an average score of ninety-six. The second place caller had a ninety-one and third place eighty-eight." She mentioned the names of the winners, and those present responded with an enthusiastic round of applause. She added the top three could say a few words if they wanted. The winner walked up to the table where he was quick to mention he was a professional guide from Wyoming. He also said the name of his outfit as well as the brand of call he used. He was full of talk and went on talking about how he enjoyed hunting turkeys, that he started hunting at a young age and subjects of little interest to those present. The second place and third place winners declined to say anything. An event officials stood by the registration table and announced, "If you-all will come up here and give Janet your number, she will give you your scores. I hope you all had fun today. See you next year."

Number fifteen was not in the top three, and his demeanor reflected a certain amount of displeasure with the day's outcome.

Janet gave me my scores which were scribbled on three pieces of paper. Apparently there were three judges. One score was seventy-two, one was sixty-five and the third an eighty-one. Mason and I walked out of the building together. On the way, I asked him how he fared. "Not very well," he said. He didn't elaborate and I didn't press him. After a few more steps he added, "I think my diaphragm call got slack. I should have brought a new one." I told him my score. He said, "Maybe next year we'll do better."

Appendix

Background Story to
So White Plus Seven

Since graduating from Carnegie-Mellon University, I completed 64 courses at various institutions of learning. The topics varied from advanced calculus to photography to French as well as a broad mix of other subjects. It would be fair to call me the eternal student. I plead guilty. I always had a curious and open mind, and I enjoyed studying new subjects. In 2015, one of the courses I took at Penn State University was titled "Introduction to Creative Writing." Several weeks into the course, the professor asked us students to write a short story based on the theme of "Snow White and the Seven Dwarfs." The story we write, he said, should be a modern-day version. The next day I wrote my story and titled it "So White plus Seven." Much to my surprise and delight, the professor as well as the other students in the class liked the piece. In fact, the professor later suggested I submit the story to an ezines. At that time, I didn't think the piece merited submittal. Nevertheless, and I followed his suggestion. Within days I had acceptances from two interested publishers. Never in the past, was any of my submittals accepted so quickly. I selected *Gravel*, the literary publication of the University of Arkansas. The piece appeared in the February, 2016 issue of the magazine. It also appeared as a reprint in the November/December, 2016 issue of *Down in the Dirt*.

In "So White plus Seven" I predicted the demise of circuses, and that prediction proved to be true two years later when the circus of Barnum and Bailey closed for good. The article pokes gentle fun at government employees. I could not resist the opportunity. My inclinations stem from my belief in less government in people's lives.

The humor of the story would best be appreciated if a reader is familiar with the original fairy tale "Snow White and the Seven Dwarfs."

Background Story to
The Metzes

Parts of the story "The Metzes" are true. As mentioned in the story, I did in fact visit the Alsace on a search although with a purpose different from that mentioned in the story; contrary to what is mentioned in the story, I was not looking for relatives. Rather, I was searching for the Fleckenstein Castle, a place where our family name, Fleckenstein, originated. The search began when I had visited a dry cleaning shop in the town of Tours, France. While in the shop, the proprietor introduced me to a Lieutenant Lang of the French Air Force who also happened to be in the store. The lieutenant, who spoke fluent English, and I chatted for a spell. After he had collected his clothing and was preparing to leave the store, he paused to ask me if I were related to the barons of the Fleckenstein Castle. I responded that I didn't know of the castle. He said it was in the Province of Alsace. He had been stationed at an airfield near the castle and that was how he came to know about the Fleckenstein Castle.

In the spring I had to travel to Germany and on the way I decided I would visit the castle that had my family name. In the Province of Alsace, I had trouble finding the castle. While searching, I asked a local if he could give me directions to the castle. Not only did he give me directions, he invited me for supper. The next day he went with me through the woods and showed me around the castle. Although he was French, he spoke only German, so we conversed in German. That visit became the inspiration for the story which is otherwise fictitious.

"The Metzes" was published in *Potluck Magazine* in February 5, 2016.

Background Story to Egyptian Pounds

"Egyptian Pounds" is a true story I experienced on one of my three trips to Egypt. I found Egypt a fascinating country occupied by varied peoples and ancient cultures. Except for the taxi drivers mentioned in the story, the people I encountered were friendly and courteous.

The story was published by *Prick of the Spindle* in 2012.

Background Story to
Too Late Dowry

In America, most of the European countries and perhaps elsewhere, couples tend to marry for romantic love. Of course, there are variations. According to the ideal scenario, boy meets girl, they date, they fall in love, and they marry. Compatibility and looks are important. A man does not expect to receive monetary compensation for taking a bride.

In some parts of the world, love between a man and a woman is not only considered unnecessary but in many ways is considered as impractical and foolish. A decision by a couple to marry is based on other considerations. Family status, a person's occupation and financial wherewithal are important. The Indian ways are an example.

If a young man is to take bride in India, he will expect to receive a dowry of some magnitude. Sometimes, a promised dowry is not paid, and the consequences can be dire for the woman.

Why did I write about Indians and their ways with dowries? First, I was an engineer with an Indian firm in Philadelphia for thirteen years and, during that time, I learned a little about the Indian ways. While Americans might find the Indian ways peculiar, it would be fair to say the Indians would say the same about Americans' marrying practices. Anyway, "Too Late Dowry" represents a story that might have taken place somewhere in India, perhaps in the not too-recent past.

The editor who accepted the manuscript for publication said he knew something about Indians and believed the dialog of the story sounded genuine. The article was published in the January 21, 2016 issue of *Out of the Gutter*.

Background Story to
Jim and the Big Black Skunk

"Jim and the Big Black Skunk" is a true story of two youths: my friend "Jim" and me. However, I must confess my friend's name was other than "Jim." The story could fairly be characterized as the behavior of two youths whose mental capabilities had not been fully developed.

Jim became a heavy smoker later in life, and I am sorry to say he died of lung cancer at a relatively young age.

The story was published by print magazine *American Trapper* in 2010.

Background Story to
A Family Affair

In my role as an engineer specializing in the design of electrical power plant designs, I spent time both traveling to the Middle East and interacting with engineers in those countries. Specifically, I was involved with plants in Egypt, Bahrain, Kuwait and Saudi Arabia. I learned that much of the Arab culture is different from ours, and many of their ways seem strange to us of the West. One of their ways are what the Arabs call honor killings. According to my understanding, a woman who is raped in an Arab country brings dishonor to her family. The customary penalty for the woman is death at the hands of a male member of the family. The death of the woman, it is said, returns honor to the family. These horrific acts are against the law, but, I've been told, they occur nonetheless. Police look the other way.

The story first appeared in *Story Shack*, an English language ezine in the Netherlands, in August, 2014.

Background Story to
A Subtle Play

Any time an individual in industry finds the opportunity for self-promotion, there will likewise be the potential for devious behavior. The book by Niccolo Machavelli provides the road guide in his book "The Prince." One might expect that when the rewards for self-advancement can be substantial, the greater the call for self-promotion.

In "A Subtle Play" I describe a scenario that might have taken place at a typical manufacturer's workplace. The story was published in September 11, 2016 in *Work Literary Magazine*, a magazine that specializes in stories about the workplace.

Background Story to
Cousin Paul

A few years ago, I discovered that I am related to Sir James Paul McCartney, the world renowned famous beetle. More specifically, Paul and I are third cousins. We both have the same great-great grandparents, one Michael Mohan and his wife whose name I have yet to learn.

Paul's grandfather, Owen Mohan, was born only a few miles from where my mother was born in County Monahan, Ulster, in the north of Ireland. Paul's grandfather very well might have gone to school with my grandparents.

I learned of the connection with Paul in part through a woman by the name of Ellen Winters who was the sister to Paul's maternal grandfather. At the time, Mrs. Winters was living alone near my Uncle Peter and Aunt Rose in Ireland. Uncle Peter said Ellen was a relation and suggested I should meet her. She invited me for tea and we had a chat.

I thought the story would make a good memoir and, so, I sent the manuscript to *Streetlight Magazine* and the editor, Susan Shafarzek, liked the story. The piece appeared in the October 21, 2016 edition.

Background Story to
Novice Bank Robber

In recent years, newspapers have been reporting weird stories about bank robberies. It seems many of the bank robbers are addicts with a wild need for cash yet foggy minds. Often the acts are carried out in an outlandish and amateurish manner. Sometimes the perpetrators are caught, but sometimes they disappear into the crowd.

The story was published in an anthology by the Greater Lehigh Valley Writers Group in June, 2015. The book was titled *GLVWG Writes Stuff* and it was made available on Amazon.

Background Story to
Pretend Love

The story was published in an anthology by the Greater Lehigh Valley Writers Group. The book was titled *Write Here, Write Now* and was made available in 2016 at Amazon.

Background Story to
We, the ROTC Cadets

The essay reports my personal experiences as a cadet at the US Army Corp of Engineers ROTC summer camp. One of the purposes of the camps is to determine if candidates are suited to be an army officer. For this reason, none of the attendees are treated with kid gloves. To the contrary, army brass hope to determine if a man can take it as well as give it. Most of the scenes reported in the story took place at Fort Belvoir, Virginia, the home base of the Corp of Engineers.

The story was published in *Military Experience & the Arts*, Spring, 2017.

Background Story to
Gobblers and Grapes

"Gobblers and Grapes" is one of eleven short stories I published in outdoor magazines. More specifically, the article appeared in the October, 1994 issue of the *Pennsylvania Game News*. Actually, the *Pennsylvania Game News* published four of my turkey stories, but I am not inclined to repeat all of the stories here.

I do not apologize for being a hunter of wild game. It was a sport that brought me out into the outdoors of Wisconsin, Ohio, Nebraska and Pennsylvania. Sometimes I was with hunting buddies. Sometimes with a dog, but often alone. If it were not for hunting, I no doubt would not have enjoyed the outdoors nearly as much as I had.

I appreciate that the typical reader of short stories may not necessarily be interested in a hunting story. Yet, I believe this story might have some appeal to the average reader. Yes, the article is about the harvesting of a wild turkey. For those persons who might be against hunting, I submit the following: The turkey gobbler of the story that met its demise at my hand had a beard that suggested it was at least three or four years old. For wild turkeys, that is a relatively long life. And it is certainly longer than that of barnyard turkeys. As turkeys go, my turkey had enjoyed a good and long life, that is, until he met me. By the way, the meat of the wild turkey is much more tasty than that of a turkey bought at a supermarket.

Background Story to
The Snow Queen Contest

Parts of "The Snow Queen Contest" are true. As suggested in the story, I was an enthusiastic skier most of my life. And at times I was also a member of three ski clubs. So, I learned a little about both skiers, ski clubs and the people who join ski clubs. One thing I learned is that skiers tend to be a lusty, don't-give-a-damn type. It could be argued that a person needs to be other than normal or pragmatic to risk life and limb sliding down steep, snow-covered, and treacherous hillsides in freezing weather.

I believe that persons who take up skiing will eventually be drawn to membership in a ski club. There are a number of reasons that make membership worthwhile. First, there are the opportunities to meet like-minded individuals—especially those of the opposite sex. There are the opportunities to partake in trips with fellow ski-nuts to distant ski slopes at attractive rates. Most ski clubs have meetings from the fall to the spring and sometimes in between. The meetings will have fashion shows, speakers, opportunities to sign-up for up-coming trips and other events of a common interest. Once a year, some clubs have a snow queen contest. The contests are intended to be light-hearted and entertaining.

"The Snow Queen Contest" was published in *Adelaide* in December, 2018. It appeared in both print and online in both the USA and Portugal.

Background Story to
Henri Rochemont

When I was in the army, I was assigned to a small US Army depot near the town of Chinon in France. I was a second lieutenant, but at the time of my arrival there were no officers' quarters. We officers were given an allowance and told to find quarters on our own. I rented a room from a family in the town of Tours, and I lived there for eighteen months. Every day I ate breakfast and supper in French restaurants and lunch at the post. Except for my time at the post during the day, usually eight to five, I lived much like a Frenchman. It was not a way of life I had chosen; it was my assignment and my duty. I had no regrets because it was an eye-opening experience and an opportunity to observe first-hand a different culture.

Except for the names, every word of "Henri Rochemont" is true. The article was published in the Winter, 2019 issue of ezine *Gloom Cupboard.*

Background Story to
Roisin

The story is entirely true except for some of the names. I did in fact have a sister who spent all of her life in the British Isles and most in Northern Ireland. I am sorry to say she passed away a few years ago and I regret that I did not have the opportunity to send more time with her and to get to know her better. That she was my sister was a family secret for many years, but in time the truth came out.

The piece was published in "Wilderness House Literary Review," July, 2021.

Background Story to
Camping with Friends

The idea for the story originated in consequence to several true-to-life events with which I became familiar. First, there are the numerous homeless people who appeared worldwide in recent years. And America, it seems, as its fair share of these unfortunate people. The sight of homeless Americans living in tents and on streets is a recent and unfortunate phenomenon. In "Camping with Friends" I try to define the course that many of these homeless individuals might have followed before deciding on a tent for a home.

Of course, a person who lives in a tent is not necessarily destitute or forced to do so. Many, it seems, go camping for the adventure it might bring. And a way to get away, so to speak, from themselves. But, there are other reasons too.

One particular camper came to mind as I wrote the story. He had been commuting with a number of other individuals to a job site where I worked along. It was said that he grew tired of the monotonous commute, and he tried camping near the job site as an alternative. It was whispered that he had been living with a house full of kids and a nagging wife. In short, I suppose there are a variety of reasons why people will revert to camping – either alone or with friends.

The article was published in both print and online in the "Schuylkill Valley Journal," Spring/Summer, 2021.

Background Story to
Little Pietro

Today, people have all kinds of pets: not only cats and dogs as in years past, but ferrets, snakes, turtles, parrots, and, yes, chickens. While some people might raise chickens as Rhode Island Reds or Leghorns for the meat or the eggs, the more common type of chicken pet are what are known as bantams.

Bantams are small chickens, and they come in a variety of sub-species. Some are docile and readily approach humans whereas others display a more independent spirit. The story talks about events that might take place when bantams are brought to a private residence in a development.

Background Story to
The Yazidis

Years ago, I walked into the clubhouse of the Milwaukee Skeet and Trap Club. That day I merely was interested in seeing the club's facilities and how they operated. In prior years I had shot trap although not at the Milwaukee club. I found the layout of the facility was different from most clubs that had skeet or trap shooting. The Milwaukee clubhouse was at the shoreline of Lake Michigan and the clay birds were launched out over the water.

While I was sitting in the clubhouse to watch shooters, there was another visitor sitting nearby. Somehow we got to talking, and somehow the subject turned to charity. The gentleman might have been a businessman with good income. He told me that he believed in charity, but he preferred to bypass the institutions that commonly received donations from charitable Americans. He specifically mentioned the American Red Cross. He said he thought their overhead was too large and that, consequently, only a fraction of the donated money goes to those who need it. No, he said, he gave directly to the people who needed it. He added that in prior years he sponsored a family from Eastern Europe. He said he paid their way to America and put them up in a house for a year. How generous, I thought. I had no reason to doubt the man. I believed he truly did what he claimed. He seemed like an honest and responsible person.

When I heard of the Yazidis and their tragic plight, I wondered if there were persons who had considered reaching out to them much as the gentleman I met in Milwaukee. Thus, my piece "The Yazidis."

Background Story to
The Twentieth Reunion

Whether it's the twentieth high school reunion or the twentieth college reunion, those celebrations always prove to be of interest to the attendees. Friends and lovers from years ago will be present. Sports heroes and cheer leaders of school years will no longer seem as deserving of the awe and respect they once enjoyed. Some women who were at one time in the wall flower category had sprouted into attractive and alluring middle aged women. Many will be thinking of the path not taken, the friendship not pursued. A mixture of surprises will be available for attendees at a reunion along with memories and perhaps a few regrets. Of course there would also be opportunities of the type mentioned in the story to renew friendships.

Background Story to
Driving to Work

Many people who work for a living find it necessary to drive an automobile to their place of employment. For those of us who perform this task, to be sure a variety of experiences may occur along the way. And, all are not necessarily pleasant. "Driving to Work" speaks to the common problem.

I maintain it is always best to find humor in the plans of mice and men as well as in the driving habits of fellow citizens. Taking seriously the behavior of other drivers on the highways can lead to heart burn, high blood pressure, disappointment and in the extreme…road rage. In the long run, it's far better for one's state of mind to assume a detachment from the observed folly on the highways. Consider the happenings on roadways with a sense of humor.

Background Story to
Sirus

The story was inspired by experiences related by a close friend of mine who both owned and raced horses. Occasionally I went to races with him. Once, when his horse won, I walked the horse around the track and to the winner's circle. My friend knew a number of both owners and jockeys at the tracks. From those sources, he had gathered an abundance of tales. A few he related to me. I learned that it would be fair to say people who bet on the ponies truly know little of the tricks devised back in the stables. Of course, the well-known advice is still valid: Do not bring to a racetrack more money than what you can afford to lose.

Background Story to
Encounter on Line Mountain

Every word of my "Encounter on Line Mountain" is absolutely true. To be sure, it was an experience I would have preferred to avoid.

While the story could be called a hunting story, it is not about shooting wild game. Rather, it is about an effort to stay alive under threatening circumstances. It was an episode when I was keenly aware that one misstep and I would be killed. It would be a death to be feared.

Background Story to
Comes Around

When I was on active duty with the US Army, I met a second lieutenant who told me his unfortunate experiences running the post's enlisted men's club. I have no reason to suspect he had fabricated the experience he related. His story proved that, as is commonly said, "What goes around…" Life is sometimes like a merry-go-round. Or, would it be appropriate to say "The chickens come to roost?" Something like that!

Background Story to
Hamburgers

Americans love their hamburgers; there's no doubt about it. Me? I have eaten hamburgers although it's been a while - at least twenty-five years. Why is that? First, I inherited a suspicion about ground meat from my mother. Also, I grew hesitant as a result of watching butchers prepare ground meat. Besides, there are too many other, more enticing alternatives to hamburgers.

The piece is based on two observed characteristics of American tourists abroad: A love of hamburgers and a reluctance to try unfamiliar dishes of a forging origin. I also sprinkled in a few noticeable characteristics of tourists. When I was a resident of France, I had the opportunity to note the behaviors and habits of a number of tourists that came from a variety of countries to travel France.

In the story, I mention the Hotel Opal. It's a delightful, small hotel on Rue Tronchet, Paris where my wife and I stayed when we visited the city.

Background Story to
The Two Mile Club

The main scene of the story is inside a nuclear power generating station. I became familiar with nuclear plants as a result of my having performed engineering for eleven of the plants as well as my having been inside nine of them. As a result of my experiences, I learned how the plants are operated and I personally witnessed the day-to-day operations of the plants. Some of that experience is reflected in "The Two Mile Club."

While at one of the mentioned nuclear plants, I spoke with a fellow engineer who told of a tryst that occurred at one of the nuclear plants. He said it took place on the night shift in a manner similar to that reflected in the story. He assured me his story was entirely true. He said he personally saw tapes of the type mentioned in the story.

Background Story to
The Late Train from Alexandria

The story is by and large true. I was in Egypt at the time depicted in the story and traveling on business. I had a hotel room in Cairo, but I had taken the train to Alexandria to resolve business matters with an associate. One thing led to another, and I found myself occupied until late in the day. To return to my room in Cairo the same day, I found myself obligated to take the late train. Earlier I had been cautioned against taking the late train in part because it made numerous stops between Alexandria and Cairo. For that reason, the trip took longer. I had also been advised to avoid second class seats, but, when I arrived at the station, I learned there were only second class seats available. I had no choice as I wanted to return to Cairo that evening. Staying overnight in Alexandria would have been inconvenient. In short, parts of the story are true. Egypt is a fascinating country.

Background Story to
The Annual Turkey Calling Contest

To persons who do not hunt the wild turkey, an event as a turkey calling contest might seem to be a bizarre happening. Be assured they do occur, and they are attended by enthusiastic participants of the sport of wild turkey hunting.

Here I represent what happens at a typical turkey calling contest. The reported events of the story are in part a reflection of true events. I have entered turkey calling contests, but, I must confess, was never a winner. The human judges thought my level of competency was not of a sufficiently high level. On the other hand, I have had success on numerous occasions with the genuine judges, namely the wild turkeys.

Acknowledgements

Book Cover Design
by
Francesca Michelon
of
MerryBoookRound
Rome, Italy

The Author

Joseph E. Fleckenstein, a graduate of Carnegie-Mellon University, lived at times in Pittsburgh (Pennsylvania), Milwaukee, Columbus (Ohio), York (Pennsylvania) and Reading (Pennsylvania). Today he lives in Maryland, a little north of Washington, DC. Over the years he has made his living as an electrical engineer involved primarily in the design of electrical power generating plants. He is the inventor of seven US patents and a number of foreign patents.

For much of his life, Fleckenstein enjoyed hunting, skiing, and running. More recently though, he spends most of his spare time reading and writing. Some of his nonfiction pieces have won awards. He has published over 40 items, most of which were short stories that appeared in print or online.

There are more particulars at the author's website, www.WriterJEF.com.